Dream Letters

Dream Letters

Angel Camacho

DREAM LETTERS

iUniverse books may be ordered through booksellers or by contacting:

iUniverse
1663 Liberty Drive
Bloomington, IN 47403
www.iuniverse.com
844-349-9409

ISBN: 978-1-6632-1051-7 (sc)
ISBN: 978-1-6632-1053-1 (hc)
ISBN: 978-1-6632-1052-4 (e)

Print information available on the last page.

iUniverse rev. date: 11/04/2020

This is for my Mother, Father and Nephew
Margarita Avila, Luis Camacho and William Camacho Nunez

To the best gift in life, My Friends
Jessica Pires
Patricia Vera
Mitzianna Rivera
Fannysha Colas
Liz Beaudoin
Esmeralda and Stephaniee
Ralphie and Nina Pagan
And
Alexander Rivera ♥

Thank you for believing in my Dreams.
Close your eyes and escape into your Dreams.

Prepare to fill your minds with twisted
endings and alternate realities.
Love – Angel Luis Camacho

Dream Letter 1
Bloodshot

I still remember the day that we tried to leave the city. Manhattan was overrun with people dying all around us every single day. We could even hear our neighbors, an elderly couple, coughing so loudly through the paper-thin walls. They seemed to sound like they were in so much pain and discomfort. One night, we all noticed there was no more coughing or any noise coming from their apartment. Every time Lilly and I asked about them, Mom and Dad would just tell us that it seemed as if they must have gotten some medicine and are probably feeling better; I bought it then since it would never enter my mind that they would be most likely dead. A day or two later, I overheard my dad on the phone with the building management telling him that someone should really check in on them. About an hour or so later, an ambulance arrived outside of our building with its lights on. I peeked out the window and saw some paramedics walking out, carrying two people in black bags on their stretcher. That's the moment when I knew that our neighbors definitely did not get better.

My mom decided she had enough trying to keep us all in this city. My parents agreed that we should try and leave Manhattan before it got worse. We all helped loading up the SUV with our family belongings. As we drove, we began to notice there were some roadblocks set up outside of the city limits to prevent anyone from traveling and possibly exposing the virus elsewhere. We tried many different ways to leave the city, but cops blocked every road possible. Every time we were stopped, the cops would tell us to go back to where we came from or we would experience problems. My mother was getting so frustrated, but she refused to give up on us, she was determined to get us away from this miserable place. She wanted her family to be in a place where we felt safe, a place where her children didn't have to hear people suffer and eventually die on the other side of a wall.

After what seemed like hours of driving, we came across a screening center for people that were trying to travel out of the state. We were forced to wait in a line for hours. The heat of the sun baked us in our car as we waited to be approved to continue traveling. Time seemed endless as we slowly inched forward in line waiting for our turn to be screened. When we finally approached the screening center at the edge of the blockade, the people working there asked us to pull into a yellow box painted on the pavement. Then they requested us all to get out of the vehicle and stand on the spots indicated next to our doors. This is when my life turned around...

One by one the medics began to test us and check our vital signs. Dad was checked first and tested out fine. The workers used a little laser to peer deep into his eye. After he was done, he came back to us. He described the experience as just feeling a slight discomfort as they ran the test to Lilly so she wouldn't worry. A little light came on the back of the machine, and the light lit up green after each of my family members were tested. Then the medic came around to my side of the vehicle. The man in what looked to be a space suit, leaned down to look me over and gave me a quick visual check. He noted that I looked clean just like the rest of my family. Another spaceman said that he had to check everyone regardless of how we looked since anyone could be a carrier. The man held the little laser reader up to my eye. Suddenly the medic paused since the small machine flashed red with an alarming little beeping noise. Instantly I saw my mom's face drop, her pupils widened as she watched them attempt to take me away. She began to scream as one of the spacemen grabbed my arm. She shouted to them that no one in my family has left the house in weeks and that there was absolutely no way I could be infected. The spaceman told her to calm down, but she just kept shouting as she struggled with them to get a hold of me. Dad was instructed to collect her, since she refused to relax.

The next thing I remember was being dragged backward by my arm, a hard hand gripping onto me tightly. I watched my mom pull away from the first man, and then push past the second man who had also tried to restrain her. Dad pushed the second man but was then promptly hit in the temple of his head with the stock of a gun. I watched as he went down like a sack of potatoes, face first into the asphalt with a sickening wet thud. After seeing that my mom still refused to surrender, her eyes were only on me, reaching out for me, screaming to give me back to her, but her open and gaping mouth screeching with motherly fear was only met with a spray of bullets from a spaceman's gun. The man shot her directly in the face. I saw the blood spray down her chest and body as they continued to shoot her lifeless soul that laid on the ground. The only reason the man stopped shooting her was because he no longer had a response from his gun. I looked at Lilly and noticed she was being dragged away to wait in a cage with no roof in the blazing New York summer sun, with all the other children who were separated from their parents.

The man pushed me onto a massive steel truck and chained me to a wall with a few other people who looked extremely sick. They looked terrible with their skin appearing grey and eyes were bright red with bloodshot. Their mouths hung open and groaned nearly constantly. I think it's probably from how uncomfortable they were. The other people in the truck didn't seem to care about me but every time the door opened and someone new was put into the truck, some of the sick people would lean towards them so they can try to touch their arms and their faces. What were they trying to do? The more people that went into the truck the more riled up the sick people seemed to become at each disturbance.

We were shipped off to a huge building. I had no idea how far we traveled since the truck didn't have any windows for me to look out of. I could only see the faces of the grey people staring at nothing the entire way. Once they brought us into the building, I was put into a cell which had a single bed and a rotten sink with a rat running around it drinking the bits of water falling from the faucet. I was given a yellow jumpsuit to wear and was told that I was expected to be on my best behavior here or I would end up like my parents. That sent a shiver down my spine. The food here was terrible, no taste or texture but it was either this or die of starvation. I tried to ask what was happening, and why I was here since I wasn't sick. Everyone ignored me and no one ever gave me a response. The only person that gave me the time of day was a woman who came around every morning to check my vitals and take some measurements of my wrist through a little scanner. She would also take notes on the status of how my eyes looked. She was kind to me; I still remember her blue eyes and waist long black hair. She told me that I was very special and that I was going to save everyone else in the building. She also said how thankful she was that I was here.

The doctors didn't seem to think that way about anyone else around here. Those who were extremely sick were taken to isolation and left there until they eventually starved. The food became less and less as more and more people arrived. I overheard some of the workers of the facility talking about denying entry to anyone else. A woman came around to my cell to take samples of my blood from my little wrist. She bruised it as she clumsily tried to take my charts to place it on the table next to the jail cell door. She said that they were going to use it to try and find a cure. Could my blood be used in some way to help people who were already sick? Could this prevent people from getting sick all together? After she completed her task, she said "thank you" to me and walked away.

I was never allowed to socialize with any of the other patients. The workers told me that they didn't want me to become exposed and all of a sudden lose my immunity to the virus and become infected too. Was that even possible? How would I know? I am an average student in the fifth grade who hates science. I preferred art after all. I was given a little piece of chalk from one of the medical technicians so that I could draw on my cell walls. They also said that I could have extra food so that I could continue making more blood for them to take daily. The food they gave me tasted like metal. They told me the food was fortified with iron so that I wouldn't feel woozy.

I drew my family on my cell wall. Dad was the tallest, he stood almost twice as tall as I was. He promised me one day I would be taller than him, but how will I ever know now? Mom was just shorter than him by a hair. She was wearing her favorite heeled sandals that allowed her to catch up with my dad. I drew myself next, making my drawing almost up to mom's shoulders, and then I drew my little sister Lilly after me. She had hair almost as long as she was tall which she kept in a silly little ponytail that flopped around whenever she walked. I picked on her a lot for that ponytail but right about now I just hope she is alive and well. I hope I can find her one day. She's all I got.

It was a late Monday evening, a few weeks after being in the jail cell, something strange happened. My breakfast was never dropped off that morning, and the kind woman with the black hair never showed up to check on me. As I laid in my bed, my stomach began to growl. All of a sudden, I swore I heard a loud growl that did not come from within me. There was always plenty of coughing, but now this was a growl. I heard that sound once before in here, but that person was taken out of their cell immediately and moved to isolation. I saw them wheel him by. He was just as grey as the people in the truck.

I jumped out of bed, slid across the floor in my yellow jail suit and looked out as much as I could out of the barred doors. I saw no one, but the growling got louder. I heard some shuffling noises and some sliding to my right towards the cell on the end of the row. I did my best to see if I could spot anything.

What I saw was a doctor - knee length white coat, blue diapers on his shoes, white gloves and a black mask on his face. He walked ever so slowly down the hall, scanning everything along the way with a slack jawed expression. Drool dribbled down his chin, soaking through the mask and his bloodshot eyes scanned over me as if he didn't even see me. I tried to talk to him, but he did not seem to hear me. He continued down the hall and stopped at the cell to my left. An older patient lived in there, he seemed healthy too; he did not understand why he was there if he was never infected before. He tried to scream at the doctor and tried to get him to let him out. He called him mean and disturbing names and reached his hand out to grab the doctor's white coat. The physician reacted so violently, more so than I could have ever imagine. He grabbed the older patient by his arm and twisted it. Then he began pulling him up off the floor where he was sitting and yanked his arm forward to his mouth. The doctor pulled the man tightly against the bars as the older man screamed in agony. I could see him trying to pull himself away from the doctor and back into the safety of the cell. The older man was screaming obscenities at the physician. Finally, the man was able to free himself from the doctor's grasp but not without sprays of blood splashing across the doc's nice white coat. He seemed outraged that the old man was able to pull away, so he launched into the bars. The only thing stopping him from ripping the prisoner apart was the physical barrier between the two. He hissed and snarled. I could hear his hands pulling and ripping at the bar, smashing his head against it as blood dripped down from his forehead. The elderly man cried and begged for help, but no one came to his rescue. The shouting drew more attention towards the people from down the hall. They all congregated at the door while screeching and hissing at the man in the cage; eventually piling onto each other. There were at least 20 people pushing onto the bars trying to get the older man. I could hear the metal creaking and the man continued to scream and plead for anyone to help.

With a sickening snap, I heard some of the bolts in the ceiling shift from the pressure of all those people pressing into the cell. After a few moments they all fell inward. At first the man screamed so loudly, then moments later the scream became wet and gargled. Then finally fell silent. There were disgusting noises coming out from the cell, and soon after, some of the people started to file out from the inward pressed bars with blood around their mouth.

One of the security officers fell with a heavy thud onto the slanted bars, causing it to spear him in the belly. I found it odd that he did not react, but instead he dragged himself forward back down the hallway to my right. The bar pulled itself through him and split his body in two, like an old banana, from the belly to his groin. He did not seem to notice, even though he could only crawl with his hands. As he passed by, I was able to reach down and grab a key ring from his belt. I saw his entrails taking a little longer to pass by my cell. He stunk.

Once I saw most of them scuffle off down the hallway, I reached over the bars so I could find which one of the big metal keys would unlock my door. I was able to find the right one and it opened with a heavy clunk. The door squeaked as I opened it and as fast as I could, I silently slid into the hallway. Peeking through the side of the wall, there were grey people all over the place, but luckily, they didn't seem as interested in me as they were with the patient next door. I was able to slip right by most of them. They only seemed to notice me if I accidentally touched them or bumped into them. Even then, they only sniffed in my direction, and could care less if I was around. It felt as if they looked through me, rather than at me.

I only had brief knowledge of how to move around in this building. I was only taken out of my cell infrequently to shower and sometimes to get my hair cut. Otherwise, I was always left in my cell. I ran towards one of the "EXIT" signs posted above a large steel door with a warning label on it. Beyond that door, there was a set of stairs that I started running down from. Another woman shoved herself past me as I tried to leave the stairway. A group of grey people were following her like predators up the stairs. When they caught up to her, they attacked her and yanked her back down to the floor level I was at. As she was dragged away, she grabbed me by my ankles and begged for me to help her. She couldn't finish her plead for help; a man grabbed her by the lower jaw and with his thumbs in her mouth, he pulled away so hard that it caused her jaw to dislocate from its place. Her eyes moved for a few seconds, but her body was still. I could see the expression on her face change multiple times as her eyes glossed over and then there was nothing left in her. They continued to drag her lifeless body down the stairs and all I saw was a bunch of these grey people feasting on her. I knew I had to escape.

I reached the lobby of the building and it was almost empty. There were barricades placed at the front door, but these actually looked like they were professionally installed. Were they trying to keep us locked up? Were we just a group of lab rats for an experiment? This made me angrier.

There were obvious signs of scuffles in the lobby. Chairs were thrown over and the greeting desk had paperwork scattered everywhere. As I approached the doorway, I noticed that there were so many bloody handprints on the glass, but when I reached up to touch them, they were all on the inside. I realized something wasn't trying to get inside it was trying to escape. I attempted to push the door open, to get some fresh air, but the door was locked tightly. It didn't move an inch in its jam. I kept jiggling it and the frustration in me was beginning to rise. I could see the outside! I was so close! I could almost smell the fresh air. I was so angry that I started to bang against the glass with the sides of my fist while shouting at the freedom just outside of it.

I heard a soft familiar voice come from behind me. I turned around to see the black-haired nurse standing in front of me. She was struggling to make sure the door stayed shut behind her. She was having a hard time, making her arms move in a way that the latch would stick. It clicked heavily, and she sighed shaking the fog out of her head. She turned my way, and I noticed that her skin was turning grey. I could see the blood dripping from her eyes, but she seemed genuinely happy to see me.

She asked me how I had made it this far? How I had managed to come all this way alone, she then stroked my hair with an awkward hand, it did not seem in full control of her. She said I reminded her of her son and that she hated seeing me cooped up in that cell. She dug oddly in her white coat pocket and handed me one last candy, a hard caramel, and wrapped it in my fingers. Then she smiled, one side of her mouth did not respond to her. In a gravely, painful sounding voice she told me that she would give me a key. She handed me a little silver key that would fit in the lock on the front door. The only thing she wanted me to do was to promise her that I would lock the door behind me and take a slip of paper that she had attached to the key. She said that the paper would keep me safe and that I would need to hurry and leave the premises. She couldn't protect me from these grey people even if she wanted too. She wouldn't stay "herself" much longer either, she was turning into them. Her leg had a bite mark with blood leaking out.

She walked away from me and slouched down to the floor. She was leaning back against the door with an exhausted look on her saggy face. Her black hair pooled around her like a tar pit. I thanked her for everything she had done for me, then I went to unlock the front door.

The lock stuck a bit, but she encouraged me ever so softly to try a little bit harder. She also told me to make sure the door closed all the way behind me once I left and to make sure I locked it once I got out. She made sure to keep repeating that so I would follow her instructions. I saw her body continuously jolt as I struggled to open the door. Finally, I turned the key and pushed the glass door open. I took one last look at her and told her she could come with me since the door was now open, but she didn't say anything. Her head hung low; she no longer lifted her chin at my voice. Instead, she smiled creepily and charged towards me.

I slammed the door shut in fear and locked it before she can break free. I can see all of the grey people running towards the door as well, but they couldn't do anything at this point since the doors were locked. I cried as I saw them violently attack each other. All they ever wanted was freedom. All of a sudden, a gas spray was released, and they all fell down one by one like a domino effect. The nurse placed her hand on the glass door and fell into a deep sleep.

I didn't know where to go so I ran over to the side of the hill against the building and sat on a rock overlooking the city. I saw a ship at a dock that was unloading large boxes with human arms sticking out, onto a ramp leading to the facility, like some sort of human cargo ship. I read the nurse's note, which you will see as the top sheet of this letter, indicating that I have COVID-19 antibodies and that I do not express symptoms of the disease. Those infected do not seem interested in me the way they did with the other patients. This is my mission, I will find my sister by curing the world, I am the key that will open the door to freedom.

Dream Letter 2
Send for Help

I should've stayed home; I should have never answered that text. I can't believe this is happening to me right now. It was ten o'clock at night when Gia texted me, she was tired of staying in, she wanted to go out and loosen up a bit which we normally did on the weekends.

I was in my dorm, studying for a physic midterm I had the next morning. My brain kept turning on and off just thinking about the devastating news my mother informed me of a week ago. She told me that she was filing for a divorce from my dad. She was tired of him leaving every weekend to these "Business Trips" and coming back home with red lipstick stains on his shirt. My parents been together for more than 20 years, and I knew that this was going to destroy our family. Dad always had a thing for the younger girls, and mom was too stupid enough to not notice it. She picked up the courage to file for divorce and Dad was becoming bitter and angry toward everyone he spoke to.

Gia insisted we should go out for some drinks, and as I told her that I was unable to go, she then said that if I wasn't out by 11pm she would be infuriated. She complained yet again that I was a terrible best friend, and she told me that I needed to escape out of this storm cloud that I had over my head.

Justin and I broke up over a month ago and I was still not over it, but I knew that maybe going out and having a couple of drinks will ease the pain away. Wrong. How stupid can I be? I laid down in my soft therapeutic mattress bed, staring into the ceiling, contemplating whether or not I should go. Justin was over me anyways, I saw him hooking up with that whore he cheated on me with, so I thought it would be best to take up on Gia's offer and head to the Club in Downtown Los Angles.

I sprinted to the bathroom, putting myself together. I threw on a silky-smooth black dress that reached just above my knees with my favorite pairs of red bottoms. I made sure my lipstick matched the bottom of my shoe. I curled my hair and made sure to run it through with my fingers to avoid any entanglements. I put on some mascara to brighten up my deep blue oceanic eyes, and then the phone rang again. It was Justin.

I ignored it and gently walked outside to meet up with Gia. I scooted into the passenger seat, and we drove away. During our drive, Gia kept on bringing up the conversation between my parents' divorce, she even said that my Dad at one point was checking her out. I almost barfed. I insisted we change the conversation, I didn't want to talk about them anymore, I wanted to dance my life away and wake up in an unknown place. I guess you have to be careful with what you wish for.

We arrived at the parking lot; That night seemed to be a special night only because the line was longer than expected. The wind blew stronger, causing my ID to fly away from my hand. A very tall muscular man with bright hazel eyes came forward to hand me back my ID. I thanked him and smiled as we approached the entrance of the club. I looked back to see if he was still staring at me and in fact he was.

Gia kept pulling me over to her and as I looked back again, he was gone. I disregarded his disappearance and walked inside the club. The music was loud; you can feel the ground shake as everyone jumped to the beat. Gia and I walked over to the bar and asked for two shots of Tequila. We were toasting to being single in our early 20's. We promised each other that we would have the best night of our lives. After one shot came another and then another. I lost count of all the tequila that was consuming my body as I ascended into the crowd losing sight of my best friend. I danced until I could no longer hold the pain on my feet. Then I felt someone press behind me, and it was the man who picked up my ID from the ground. As I lifted my hands in the air, he slowly placed his palm on my waist. I can feel the steadiness of it as I quickly turned around to face him. He smiled and I quickly glanced away, I can feel my cheeks burning from all the blushing. He came close to my ear and told me his name was Alberto and that he was visiting from Spain. He told me I was the most beautiful women in the club, he asked for my name and in return I told him my name was Stephanie.

The DJ announced last hour for all drinks at the bar. Alberto offered to buy me a drink, so we both walked to the nearest bar. He ordered Jack Daniel and I insisted we should do Tequila, I didn't want to mix drinks, but he reassured me that I would be okay and to trust him. How stupid was I! In an effort of looking for my friend, he took the drink and forced it down my throat. Some of the alcohol drooled from the side of my lip, but he held my chin upwards and told me to swallow. Now he was talking dirty just how I like it. Within seconds I saw Gia down the hall with a man herself, she looked at my direction and motioned with her face that she was dying to kiss him. I giggled. Alberto asked me what was so funny, and I told him about Gia and her little crush down the hall. He chuckled and said that the man down the hall was his younger brother Julian.

We both walked towards Gia and Julian to introduce myself. Julian was a lot more handsome; his eyes were green, smooth olive skin gleaming in the lights as it shined directly at him. His smile was bright, and his teeth were as white as snow. I extended my arm for a shake, but he launched at me, to only plant two huge kisses on both sides of my cheek. He kept on repeating that his brother was a keeper, I chucked as Alberto walked me away from them to not interrupt any longer.

My head kept spinning; the room felt as if it were falling on me. The club was enlarging, the hallway seemed endless and then I knew something was wrong. Alberto's face resized like a balloon. He asked me if I was okay, his voice sounding so distant, slower than usual, and as the speed of light I was gone.

It felt like an eternity. My head felt heavier than before, and it took me longer than usual to open up my eyes. In every attempt to open them up they burned just a little more. After coming full to my senses, I realized that I was tied up inside a van. My arms and legs bound to a zip tie. I tried to scream but was only matched with a gag in my mouth. Tear fell down my eyes as I attempted to force the zip tie loose. It only made it worse causing me to bruise my wrist. As I looked around me, I noticed Gia was sitting right across from me, still in a deep sleep. I also noticed a bunch of other girls from different nationalities with their makeup smeared down their face. They were all bruised up, some cried others didn't. I wondered "where the fuck can I be?". The driver of the van made a harsh stop, causing Gia to swing face flat to the ground, she woke up and attempted to scream but all you heard were muffles. She looked at me with regrets. We both knew this was a huge mistake.

The door of the van opened, shinning the light into all of our faces, we flinched like vampires in daylight. A huge shadow hid the light and as I looked up, a tall massive man came inside the van pushing the van lower to the ground with his weight. He had 666 tatted down across his left cheek and he smiled viciously at us. He wore a tore up tank top and he reeked like a dead horse. He spoke to the driver in Spanish and they motioned at us flickering their tongues through their fingers. The man in the back of the van, grabbed Gia and examined her body. He touched her breast, and then he licked her face.

In a fit of protective rage, I was able to stretch out and kick the man in the back of his knee, sending him face first into the van wall, a loud metal thud echoed in our cage and the other girls glared at me, eyes filled with fear. The large man got up and turned on me quickly, drawing a massive hand across my face so hard, that I couldn't even feel the pain from the slap. It rammed my head into the opposite wall, and the last thing I could hear was Gia shrieking into her gag as he cut her face with a pocketknife. Everything went dark for me again.

When I woke up, I was inside the warehouse, I was locked in a tiny little cell, with other white girls with blonde hair. There were three of us. Gia was across from me in a cage with a few other Asian girls. I could see other cages set up as well. When I tried to go to the other side of our cage, I was restrained, my bound wrists were also tied to one of the bars. The girl next to me seemed hurt, her leg almost looked to be at an angle with her shin not being straight. She was slouched into the corner and didn't seem responsive.

Some time passed and we could see that morning was just beginning. As the sun came up, more men who spoke multiple foreign languages came into the building and brought other people with them. These other people didn't fit their aesthetic. They were cleanly dressed, neatly put together. I heard one of them speaking to what seemed to be one of our handlers and ask him if we would be prepared by evening for "showtime", and the handler positively agreed.

I was dragged into the bathroom by a handler and thrown into an icy cold shower, my body shivered as I attempted to wash up quickly, the only thing keeping me warm were the tears falling from my eyes. The shower stopped and I was then slammed to the ceramic tile wall and patted dry. In his attempt to pat me dry he placed his hand down to my butt and in rage I kicked him in the balls. All of that to be greeted again with a fist straight to my mouth. My lips cracked as blood dripped down to my chin, in an aim for a second fist, he was stopped by a woman. She yelled at him and told him to stop immediately. She couldn't afford her guest to drop their price on us, they expected beauty and elegance, not a rag doll. He stared down at me in disgust and walked away. I fell down to the ground and cried louder. The woman came close to me, squatted down and said, "It'll be over quicker than expected, just comply with their demand", she lifted herself up and walked away.

I thought about my parents at the moment. Are they searching for me? Why would they, they're more worried about who's getting what from this divorce rather than their own daughter.

After my brutal shower, I was given some clothing and told to wear it or go naked. He tossed me over a ragged crop top with loose edges; its V neck cut deeply down between my breasts. I was not allowed a bra. I was also given a lacy pair of black panties that attached to stockings that came up just above my knees. I was also then expected to jam my feet into platform stilettos that didn't fit me at all... once I put on this outfit, I felt terrible. I knew that I was being used as an item, and I could feel everyone's eyes on me. Once dressed, I was shoved back into my cage for what felt like an eternity while all the other girls were also cleaned and dressed.

Sunset seemed to come so early, and it drenched the inside of the warehouse in a molten gooey light. The men who were supervising us started to take each of us, one by one out of our racially organized cages. The big man who bathed me grabbed my upper arm and dragged me from the cage, barely letting my feet touch the ground as I was pulled towards the door. I begged him to let me go, I just wanted to go home, but he didn't listen to me, no one did. I wasn't treated as a person. No one saw me that way. It was terrifying.

I was shoved into a tiny room that was only large enough for one chair; the door took up one wall, while the opposite wall was a pane of glass that I could only see my reflection in... I looked like a slut, my hair was a mess from being pushed and pulled around all day. I had some red marks from the man's knuckles on my face. My outfit was terrible. I couldn't help but cry, hot tears poured down my face as I tried to cover my body as much as I could, curling into a ball on the chair. The little black room was dimly lit by a showroom light casting a golden beam directly on me as if I were a product on a shelf. After a few minutes I could hear the other rooms being filled with girls of other nationalities, I could hear more men's voices enter the hallway which the glass looked into. As I got close enough to the glass, I could see through to the girl across the hall from me. It was Gia! I could recognize her gorgeous black hair and milky white skin anywhere... she wore a lavender baby doll dress with thigh high stockings on, no shoes, her feet were just accentuated by the stockings.

A group of men started coming down the hallway, talking amongst each other about the girls they had just finished viewing. They made lewd comments, letting each other know what they would do to us if the glass was not in the way... finally, after a few minutes they got to me, and the first man banged on my glass with a fist covered in gaudy golden rings, it scared me so badly I flung back to the chair and clung to it as if I was sitting on a cliff. They all laughed at me, called me a "scared slut", and said how great it would be to "break me in" especially because I seemed so young...

So many men passed by my cage. I couldn't see all of their faces, there were so many who had come to view all of us in our captivity. Finally, the last few men passed. They looked drunk, and stumbled through the hallway, smearing themselves against the glass. One of them had his penis in his hand, and drug it across the glass of my enclosure, motioning to me with his tongue out. His friend pulled him along and told him they would be late, and that they wouldn't get a room if he wasted their time.

Again, one by one we were dragged out of our rooms and forced into a holding pen - a black room filled with chairs. Every once in a while, a man would come and pull one of us out, the girl who was chosen would never come back inside. We couldn't hear anything, so I had no idea what was taking place behind those doors...

Once my time came, the man grabbed me by my hair, and yanked me from the room. I was outside in a big white room, the majority of the warehouse had individual rooms that were covered out with black curtains. Inside of them they looked pitch black. I could see other girls, fully naked, standing outside of these black rooms, trying to hide themselves with their hands. When selected, they were forced into the room. Some would come out quickly, others wouldn't come out, at least that I could see.

I was made to stand in front of a room, the man pulled my clothing off of me, and I was forced, just as the others were, to stand naked in front of the room that I was assigned to go in; a girl had entered the room minutes before it was my turn. Shortly after, she exited hastily, tears in her eyes and sobs in her throat as she continued to hide herself with her hands. She was quickly grabbed and thrown into the next room.

I was then shoved into the room that she had just exited. The man inside the room growled past me, stating that he hoped this one would be more interesting as he wasn't having a good time.

I couldn't see anything but what I thought were shapes, maybe his shoulder? Maybe the shape of a face? I felt hands grab me as the man told me to get my ass over to him. His grip was strong, and he turned me to face him. His hands roamed my body, cupping my breasts and weighing them in his palms. I tried to smack his hands away, but he grabbed my flesh and twisted it cruelly between his knuckles, making me twinge in pain. He told me to shut up and stay still, he didn't pay for a fight.

His hands continued to roam, they felt my stomach and seized up my belly. He pressed firmly against my lower abdomen, and then he shoved his hand between my legs; I screamed. I tried to hug my knees tightly together, but he slapped me sharply in the head, forcing me to raise my hands from protecting myself. The man sounded displeased, and I heard him click a button. A little red light brightened the room, and then he shoved me out. I was forced back into the big pit area, and back into the hands of one of the handling men.

He dragged me down the aisle we were in and we waited for a girl to exit another room before shoving me in. I lost my footing and fell into the darkness, my knees hitting the hard floor loudly, my face planted to the ground. Before I could get up, the man inside the room was already on top of me.

His hands grabbed my waist, feeling my body and gripping my butt tightly, touching every inch of me, he shoved his hands between my legs as well, forcing me over on my back, touching me so inappropriately I could only cry out for help. This seemed to make him happy, and his hands dug deeper into me, tearing me apart. I shrieked, until I heard the same little click of a button as I did in the previous room, hoping he would let me go, it instead glowed green. The lights in the room turned on. One of his hands were still on me, forcing his fingers into me. I tried to squirm away before realizing who was in this room with me.

The man with his fingers shoved into my body was my father. I looked up into his face and he stared down at me. The craze lust in his eyes soon shed itself into terror, and he reeled away from me just as quickly as I did from him, I screamed and screamed at him, and then he grabbed me.

He hollered as he shoved us both out of the room, I couldn't stop shaking, I was sobbing uncontrollably, he continued to shout if anyone knew who I was, but no one responded.

The woman came by and told my father, that no one was interested in his ramblings, if he didn't want me, he could've pressed the red button to release me and someone else could have used me for their own sexual desire. In anger my father pulled out his gun from his waist band and pointed it to the woman's face, he told her to say another fucking word and he would blow out her brains. Shoving me toward the exit my father kept the gun pointing at her. Two bodyguards came tolling at us and all I heard were gun shots fire, my dad pushed me out of the entryway and rushed me toward the railing, we ran into the woods. After what felt like hours of running, he handed me his trench coat that fell below to my knees, my body kept shivering, my foot bleed from the debris that were on the ground. Dad held my hand and promised me that we will get away.

We were then met at an end point, a cliff, staring straight down to the ocean. The waves crashed as they hit the rocks underneath us. We spotted a cave and Dad made me go first, instructing me to hold on to the rocks as I climbed down the cliff. A shot was fired, and Dads body fell effortlessly down the cliff, hitting his head on a massive rock underneath me. His head bleed out as I screamed for him to not leave me alone. My body fell down, crashing onto the thick wet sand. I ran toward the cave and hid there. The cave is where I am hiding now, and I write this letter in hopes that someone will find it sooner than later. I hope I can make it out of here alive. Dad had a bank statement in his pocket with his CEO pen in which I am writing this on. I hope I can escape, but for now all I can do is watch my father's lifeless body being dragged away by the ruby bloody waves that crashes ashore. If you are reading this, I might be dead. My name is Stephanie Chapman.

Dream Letter 3
Suicide Letter

I cannot deal with this kind of treatment. All my life, I have been bullied for being who I am. I have been beaten, made fun of, screamed at just for being Mexican.

As a little kid I was always teased, and kids constantly asked me why my skin looked burnt. This predominantly white neighborhood was terrible for me. I was the only kid that wasn't white on the playground. I didn't have any friends, so it made me really upset that no one invited me to their birthday parties. I remember I almost had a friend - a little girl with curly red hair. We played all day long on the playground and we got along very well. Her father was on his phone most of the time, so he didn't pay mind to what she was doing, but when he finally noticed her playing with me, he yanked her away and screamed at my mom, telling her to not let me near his daughter ever again. They left, and I never saw that little girl again...

In the fourth grade I was beaten so severely for being an "illegal immigrant". The kids dragged me over to the jungle gym and kicked me until I was unable to stand up. They yelled at me about going back to where I was from, that I wasn't wanted here and that if I wasn't born in America, I shouldn't be here. I tried to tell them that I WAS born here, I was born in a hospital just the town over. I was born in this country - I am a citizen! But they wouldn't listen. Nothing ever made them stop. That beating broke two of my ribs and caused my two-front teeth to chip. My parents did not have the money to fix my teeth, so then I was picked on for that.

In the 6th grade I was tortured for being Mexican in an all-white school. The other kids would report me to the principal for doing or saying things that I did not commit... I was called down to the office so many times for an "investigation" that they stopped calling my parents, and just told me to go home. I received immediate in school suspension for the first few weeks. No matter how hard I insisted that the other kids were lying, they never took my side of the story, instead they told me why I was so "angry". One girl reported that I touched her, and that she was afraid that I would hurt her, insane part of it all is that I never knew her. Parents came into the school at one point to complain about me, saying that their children did not feel safe in the school.

My parents were called in for a parent teacher conference with the other parents; I was also there. They said that they were disgusted by my behavior - behavior that I didn't even have! They said that I was bringing down the quality of their children's education and that it would not be tolerated. I wasn't wanted here. If I was not removed from the school some of the parents would stop donating their money. The school administrator politely asked my parents to remove me from the school, have me transferred somewhere else. When my parents denied their response due to the other schools being far away from our neighborhood, the school then told them that it wasn't their problem and that they would have to figure it out or I just wouldn't get an education.

My parents eventually found me a new school after I missed almost an entire year. I was accepted in and for a while it was fine, then the bullying started all over again. I was called "dirty" and the kids all asked me if I bathed. I showered every day; I don't know why they kept calling me such terrible names. I was completely unable to disprove anything they were saying, and it was so scary going into school every day knowing that these kids could assault me at any time. Eventually, they started being the same. I was beat up a few times by some of the sporty kids, but nothing as bad as the first time I was beaten up. I didn't think anything could be more brutal than that, except I was kept out of everything that I thought I would enjoy. I was not allowed into any clubs because no one would take me into their group, so the administrators advised me to "try again at the beginning of the next semester". They never told me how, when or gave me any opportunity.

I am sick of being treated this way. My parents came to the United States for a better life. They did cross the border into this country to avoid war and terror in their own. They came here to work hard. My father moves around a lot - which I was also picked on for - because he has to follow crop harvesting patterns during agricultural seasons. My mother worked at a local shoe factory just down the road from my school. She worked so many long hours that I was often home alone. Without the company of my family, I often created negative thoughts in my head about ending my life altogether. I cried most nights just thinking about the damage I would leave behind.

Mom, Dad, I am sorry for what I need to do. I cannot apologize enough for the pain that you will feel. I know that I am your only child; they say the loss of a child is the worst pain in the world - something no one should ever have to feel, but I cannot do this anymore. I cannot wake up in the morning and be told how worthless I am from every single person I interact with. The news states that I am unwanted. They have made statements about how Mexicans, regardless if we are legal citizens or not, are not wanted because of our brown skin and how we steal everyone else's' jobs. They blamed us for the lack of employment opportunity for other white Americans, despite the fact that the jobs that illegal immigrants do are menial, unskilled labor, that anyone can do. No education or training is needed. Why do they complain, because they aren't getting a job, that they didn't want in the first place? This world is consumed by terrible people, and I no longer want to be apart of it.

I am sorry that our president declares that my life is not worth belonging to me. I was told that I need to be on the other side of some massive wall. Some enormous structure made by God that would keep out all of America's problems like rapists and murderers. Why did they care about rapists or murderers coming across the border when they already elected a rapist to office. That obviously isn't the problem with Mexicans since Americans seem to love rape, murder and extortion more than any other country I have ever heard of. I do not want to live in a world like that. I do not want to live in a world where the leader tells people that they should hit me. Kids already hit me so hard, imagine the treatment I would experience as an adult.

Often, when my parents and I run errands in different stores, we are treated differently. The workers stalk us more than the customers. I think they are worried that because we are Mexican, we will steal from them. I cannot go into a store and mind my own business without having eyes on me and already being accused of stealing something…

Police beat Mexicans up just because of the way we look. Our nonviolent crimes are met with pure violence and hate, as if someone told the police that every Mexican person is ready to kill them at any second, why do they think we are so dangerous? I saw on the news where Mexicans would be thrown in the most dangerous of jails just because "that's where they belonged". Is that true? Do I belong somewhere dangerous and deadly? That isn't the kind of world I want to be in but seems to be the only one that is out there for me.

This is my last entry into my journal. This was the only place that I could ever go to where I knew I would not be judged. No one would beat me up, no one would judge me. This is my safe place. I love this journal, and this is the last page on it, so this is the last page of my life.

In the 7th grade, I have been harassed and I think that I will not be able to stay at this school for much longer. The kids are becoming so violent and the school is tired of dealing with me and the problems that I apparently cause. Maybe all of this could be my fault? Maybe I shouldn't have been born this way - I didn't have a choice.

I want my mother to not cry when she finds me. I want her to know that I have gone to a happier place. No one can hurt me anymore, wherever I go, even if it is nowhere. No one can call me names there, no one can tell me I am worthless because of the skin I'm in, I can't wait to experience that peace and safety... Do you think it will be soft? Warm? I am excited to know.

I want my father to know that I was weak. They have lived a life of struggle, more so than I ever could endure. He has been the backbone for his entire family for as long as he has been alive, something I will never be able to do. I want him to know that his son was a coward; I will never have the chance to grow up and disappoint him further. He will never have to see his adult son cry because I cannot tolerate the pressure of being judged for my nationality- the words will not get kinder as I get older, they are only as soft as they are now because I am a child, and minority children deserve at least some kindness.

Please know that I do not mean to hurt you. Please know that the things that I say are all true and I know you tried your best to help me. Please know that I appreciate all the effort you put into building up my life, and I am sorry if it was all a waste.

Please have me cremated, so that the dirt does not know what color my skin is. I do not want where I lay forever to know who I truly am, I do not want people who dig me up in a thousand years to know what I am. I want to leave this behind me and finally be free.

America is supposed to be the land of the free and home of the brave, but the only way for me to be free is to be brave. I have to make this next step...

I am a bit scared just looking at the rope swing by gently, I hope its quick and not painful.

I'm sorry for the rambling. I had to get all of this off my chest. Thank you for reading my last journal entry, and please try to smile in the future, smile because I was unable to. I love you both, thank you for all that you have done. Goodbye.

Dream Letter 4
The American Hero

I did three tours in Iraq and Afghanistan during the heat of a desert storm, I was in the air force and we were a part of the groups responsible for dropping bombs to weed out terrorists and evil people. It was a great experience. Sure, I still get the nightmares. Sure, I still can't tolerate loud noises. Would I ever do it again? Of course I would, anything for my country.

I was some backwoods kid, no money, no daddy, no nothing. Without going into the air force, I would have stayed a nothing just like everyone else around me. I wanted to make momma proud, I wanted to make my hometown proud, and by joining the air force, I did. When I returned home from my tours I was always greeted with banners and pretty girls welcoming me home. My family always crowded around me and I was always a name of mention in football games. It was great. I wouldn't trade that for anything in the world. All of the lives lost were worth my moment in the spotlight, and those weren't meaningful lives anyway - terrorists don't deserve to live.

I started flying planes for civilians about two years ago. I couldn't pass the mental exam for a fourth tour, they said that I had become callous and biased to the topic of interest, to the people and the environment which I was being injected into. They said that they were concerned about me not taking my teammate's lives into consideration - how could they accuse me of something like that? My teammates were Americans! The best teammates to have in the world! How could I not think about them and their wellbeing? We all had an American Dream.

Last night we flew into Dubai, we delivered a bunch of first-class ninnies from NYC to do business in some massive office building. When we arrived, we were stunned to see the infrastructure. It really was something, I had never seen anything like that before. I thought the only thing these Muslims were capable of creating were crock pot bombs and hovels in the sand - this was about as far away from a hovel as it got. We didn't have anything this impressive in the USA. Our buildings were not massive chrome towers tall enough to spit in God's face. These overshadowed everything we had back home, and it makes me so angry to think about it. The same people that I burned, bombed and blew up are over here with better things that they didn't work for. Spending American money to create more massive high rises? More expensive cars? More gold-digging wives? Whatever.

I decided I was sick of this... this atrocity on the American way. These Muslims only know how to take from us, and that's all they do - take, take, take, take. Look at what they have now! We should have this money, this prosperity! Well, I am going to take this away from them. People home will be blessed to know of the deed I've done here. I want to make a statement that all awards written in my name are set to go to the VA to help other veterans so they can make the same choices and continue to better their country after the forces are no longer with them. I want my daughter to go to college for free - she can have my tuition grants; Lord knows I've never used them. My daughter's mother ain't getting a god damn dime - tell her she can go back to the sewer with the other alligators.

When this plane completes its first turn around, I have it programmed to aim directly at the Burj Khalifa - the largest tower in this damned city. This silver bullet will hit at approximately 9:30am, and there are roughly 230 passengers on board, all Muslims from this destitute country. I am the hero the USA needs right now; I am ridding the world of these terroristic monsters.

Its high business at this time, and that building will be full when impact occurs. I wish I could be able to see it on the news and see how they praise me for doing what is needed to be done to these terrible people. They sit behind me, almost 10 feet away, and have no idea that I am going to stop them in their tracks, just how they stopped us on 9/11. Now they will see what it means to taste American Fury. I am the true American Hero... Find this letter to start the discovery of my legacy in the black box, then you will truly know what it means to live through the eyes of a hero...

Dream Letter 5
Who Killed Michael?

We always had our issues, Michael and I. He was a great man but my rage? Sometimes it went a little unchecked… Back in the good ol' days, one time after a night of drinking with some friends, Michael got on my last nerve, and I turned around and caught him with the side of my fist. That little man launched into the side of a wall, breaking his jaw and all, as if I were some big-time boxer - that isn't the case here. I got a little angry, was it wrong? Yeah, of course it was wrong. Well, little enough to say no one was going to tolerate me smacking someone else around, so the cops were called. Michael was taken away to the hospital to have his jaw wired shut for three weeks and I was sentenced to a year in prison - Michael was always too kindhearted to people who didn't deserve it, myself included, and didn't press charges.

I spent one whole year, 365 days, behind bars. I wasn't given any time for parole; I wasn't given any kindness from any of those law-making folks. Other criminals? Some dude stabbed his pregnant girlfriend in the belly and got out two months early for 'good behavior'. I punched my husband once in the head, never caused a ruckus in the cell, and I was told there would be no chance for leniency on my behalf. Other guys beat each other up - I even got my ass handed to me once just because I looked gay. Everyone seemed to have a disagreement with a gay man in jail. There's always something they just don't agree with - most of the time it's just with you being alive. So, yeah, I got beat up. I got spat on, I got cursed at and once I almost got stabbed. I had my dinner stolen a few times because they said that no gay man's mouth should be filled with anything other than dick - just the way he wanted it. I ended up not eating for three days because that joke took longer than average to die.

So, my 365 days passed pretty quickly once I got used to the harassment and neglect. I wasn't a bad man deep in my core, I wasn't cruel, I wasn't spiteful. What I did was wrong, and as soon as I got out, I sought help from a counselor that took their time to talk to me and treat me like a normal man - not a gay man. Not a man fresh out of jail. Just a man, trying to make himself better so that the world around him doesn't go to shit... I got my anger checked out, and they even gave me a few pills to help my emotional side out, now that I was classified as "dangerous". It helped to "even me out" or so they said. But it worked.

A few months after getting done with counseling and making sure all of the lessons and medicine stuck, I somehow drummed up the nerve to message Michael again, I thought, what more could happen? We were married, we are still married, I never received documents in the mail that said we weren't married anymore, so I messaged my husband. He didn't message me back right away; I think he let me stew overnight with a response. I watched my phone constantly in that timeframe, waiting for him to say something, anything, but I didn't hear from him until the next morning.

He said we could meet up for coffee, how cliché. That day we met at his favorite coffee shop - it was actually the place we had met. I was the barista there when I was still trying to afford my way through college.

We sat at the table; He was as solemn as stone, he talked for a long time about all the medical and therapeutic help he had to go through to get to where he was now - being attacked by a spouse affected him mentally, apparently. We agreed that I was at full fault, of course, and he said that I could come back to the house if I allowed him to check out my records from the counselor. I agreed. I wanted to go home.

The months went by very rapidly being back at home, and soon it started to feel like the whole thing never happened. We were having a great life together, back in the saddle as they say, right? We worked, went out for dinner, and one day we even went out for drinks with some friends again. They all seemed leary. That made sense at the time. We both drank, but I made sure to only have a few drinks after over a year of sobriety. I was a lightweight now and I could feel my head spinning. We went home that night, I had an early shift the next morning and I refused to wake up with a hangover. We both passed out in bed waiting for the next morning.

When I got up, I was pretty groggy. After drinking a glass of water, I slammed it next to the bed and went on my way to get ready for the day. I put on my factory-job uniform and went into the bathroom to put myself together and brush my teeth. While I was in the bathroom, I heard a weird noise coming from the bedroom across the hall, where Michael was still sleeping. I assumed it was our dog Coco doing something stupid, he enjoyed removing the blankets from the bed and piling them on the ground to lay on it. I paid no mind to the noise coming from the bedroom, I was more focused on getting myself together before heading to this long of a hell shift.

Making sure I looked extra spiffy in the mirror, I went to give Michael a kiss goodbye before I went off for the day, but when I touched his cheek, it was cold. He didn't move or respond to my goodbye wish. I thought, 'maybe he was just in a really deep sleep?'. He did drink a lot last night after all. I shook him gently, trying to get a little bit of a rise out of him, but nothing stuck. He didn't move at all. I didn't even see the blankets rise and fall from his chest.

I screamed at him, shook him a bit harder to try and wake him up - I thought he still had to be sleeping, right? Wrong. After a few minutes, he didn't respond to anything, I called 911. EMT came and tried to bring him back, they put him on the floor where they could pound on his chest really hard. They were being so rough on him, I thought for sure his chest would break like an old watermelon but still they attempted to revive him. Not one muscle in his body reacted, he never moved again. I was pulled aside, bawling and crying like a child as I saw my spouse being zipped up in a black bag like some kind of luggage. I could barely keep myself together.

The police officer interrogated me and asked me why I killed my husband, in attempt to reply, another officer read my mandarin rights and exposed my wrist. Of course, I was stunned, I was humiliated. What could they have meant by that, me? I killed him? I told them exactly what happened, I was just in my bathroom, heard a funny noise and that was it. What else can I say, I didn't see this coming in a million years. Fuck the cops.

They said, due to my past record of violence, and how hungover I was, they suspected me to have committed the crime. My fingerprints were all over the scene - of course they were! It was my fuckin' bedroom! I lashed out, wrongfully, but I was just so hurt. My husband laid dead, being carried out in a fucking black bag, and now I am being told I did it!

I was taken away that morning in handcuffs, in front of all of my neighbors who had come out to stick their noses into someone else's business. I was dragged into the cop car, nothing different from the year prior, and taken away to instantly be placed in a holding cell for determination.

My trial came on so fast, far too fast for a normal murder case. Normally it can take years for this kind of thing to get through the system, but this only took about a week. I tried to call every lawyer I could, to help me, but none of them wanted anything to do with some gay man who killed his husband - what black mark that would be on their portfolio. I pleaded and eventually got a public defender assigned by the state, and when we went to go sit in front of the judge, I could've sworn he used his finger to pick his nose more than pointing out the facts. The judge sentenced me to death, I was obviously a "danger" to society. That's all it took to sentence a man to death was one week in a holding cell and some rookie fresh out of college using his internship to get people killed.

I was immediately transferred to an institution where they house dangerous criminals and from that point on, I was treated like a dog. I was kept in solitary for a very long time and was told it could be years for my day to finally come and I wouldn't be given the kindness of knowing when my time was up. That was probably the worst part. I could be living my last day, and not even know it.

Every day looked the same, trapped in the gray cell walls with the thick steel door separating me from everything else that this world could offer me. They never did catch Michael's killer, which only ingrained my sentence further. No plead or appeal that I could make was ever acknowledged and half of the time I never heard a response. The other half was just people telling me that they were happy that I was on death row, and the likes of me were gone.

I write this letter to you, to tell you one last thing, I did not kill my husband Michael. Today as I was given my last meal before my death sentence, Officer Cooper came in and sat down with me for a while. He told me how excited he was that I would be gone today, he had been waiting for this day for over two years now. Officer Cooper confessed that he killed Michael, he told me that while I was in the bathroom putting myself together, he placed a gag over Michaels mouth and strangled him to death with wire cables. He told me these exact same words "You should have seen the look on his faggot face, his eyes pleaded for help as I strangled him to death. Now my neighborhood will never see another faggot again. Thank you for making my job easy, all it took was your wrongdoing of hitting him to catch a criminal case to now blame you for a crime I committed".

He referred himself as God, and that he had placed judgement on us, that's why he killed Michael.

I will tape this letter to the bottom of the tray of my last meal, in hopes he won't see it and my story will come out some day after I am gone. I just hope that Michael is on the other side waiting for me, and that he doesn't blame me too much...

Dream Letter 6
Family Business

Papa always treated me well, I thought. We lived in a little house at the end of a long dirt road, a road so long I couldn't see anyone else on it; there were no houses, no neighbors, no kids to play with. It was far away from everything, just like papa wanted it to be. The house was so tiny, I thought that it just seemed that way because I was tiny too, but it really only was one room to make up our living, sleeping and eating room - there were a few closets - and then a bathroom in the back. The floorboards were always so rough on my bare feet and legs, papa had to buy me slippers so I can avoid getting more splinters. The slippers were so warm and cozy... They were plush and shaped like little rabbits! I had never seen a rabbit before that, they must have been really cute to make slippers out of them...

The house was a little drafty, most of the windows had no glass in them. Papa would bring down fluffy blankets to sleep in during the winter months, when the air was so crisp and painful against my skin. There were some gaps in the boards that made up the walls and because of that, little creatures will come in at night in search of food. I would play with the little animals that papa caught in the traps he placed around the house. Some had long hairless tails, some were puffy. Papa said that I could never name them because these little animals came to us since they wanted to be eaten for dinner. It was a little sad that they never wanted to stay and play, but I enjoyed petting their soft fur while papa got them ready to go into the soup.

I didn't have any kind of friends. There was no one around to play with besides papa and he was always so tired from working all night, so I had to make my own friends. I made friends out of sticks that would fall from the roof, or I weaved little friends out of blades of grass when papa would let me go outside on sunny days. They were my best friends! We would talk for hours and hours about anything in the whole wide world and they told me all sorts of interesting things, and secrets too! You would never know the secrets that the grass hears because people don't think it's listening. Sticks too! They can see for miles and miles at the top of an old oak tree, they have told me the things they see, the stuff they have watched and told me stories about the world, things I could have never imagined. Sometimes the little animals would try to talk to me, but only in hisses and squeaks that I did not understand. Those were not good conversations, and I did not like talking to the little animals. I much more preferred when they were quiet on the table with papa.

I loved the quiet. Papa was always quiet. During the day, I also had to stay quiet to make sure that I did not wake him up. He slept on a mattress in the corner and I was allowed to play nicely with my toys as long as I stayed quiet. What he didn't know is that I made so much noise! I was cheering and laughing and having a great time in my head, sometimes I would just lay on the floor and stare at the ceiling and have such a wonderful time, I didn't need toys to have fun! At nighttime papa left for work and it was quiet anyway.

One night, someone came by looking through the window while papa was away, so I did what I was told to do, hide in the closet and be silent, and I was really good about it. Papa said that I did a really good job hiding away from intruders, he was so proud of me. To reward me for being so still, and so good, the next morning he brought me home a stuffed rabbit! It was so warm, so beautiful, and almost as big as I was! I was over the moon with happiness. Rabbits really are wonderful…

Papa never told me what he does for work; Every morning, I would hide in the closet until I heard a whistle, indicating that it was safe for me to come out. I kept my ear close to the door however, just to listen to the tools in his bag jump up and down as he headed to the basement.

I still remember how I found out what papa did for work.

One night, I heard a strange noise coming from the backyard, it sounded like old leaves being crushed by an anonymous footstep. In fear I ran into the closet to hide. I locked the door shut and began to count up to ten just to calm my nerves. A loud slamming could be heard from the front door, I grabbed rabbit and held him tightly, close to my heart for protection. I heard a woman scream for help; I got up from the floor and approached the door, I saw papa dragging a woman from the living room down to the basement, her hands holding tightly to the edge of the wall, making every effort to escape. Papa then whacked her in the head with a hammer as he dragged her down the basement. Blood was smeared across the floor as her hands effortlessly fell to the ground.

After a couple of minutes, I heard papa yell down from the basement and the same woman ran up the stairs trying to escape, she saw me from the keyhole and ran towards my door, she opened it up and begged me to help her. A large shadow came across the light; it was papa, he held her mouth shut and sliced her neck open with a butcher knife. Her blood sprayed me in the face, her eyes rolled back, and her hands let me loose. Papa squatted down and looked me in the eyes and said, "She is a monster, and this is what I do to monsters who try to take you away". Papa was my hero. I couldn't wait to be just like him. He took off his shirt and rubbed the blood out of my face. Then he dragged her body down the stairs and told me to help him clean up the mess. Finally, something I can help him out with.

After that night, men would start coming to the house every once in a while, picking up packages from papa. They would grab Styrofoam boxes that seemed heavy, even to papa, and take them away in another big truck - even bigger than his! One night, when I was allowed to be out in the room while papa worked, one of the men who came to pick up the packages asked papa how much he wanted to take me off his hands! Can you believe that? They wanted to buy me with money from papa! I would never let that happen. He told that man no, no one could have his little girl, no one could have his pride and joy, his protege, and he told that man to take his last box and leave. The man gave papa some money for the boxes like they always did and left the house as quickly as he could - they were scared! I know he would never sell me; I know my papa would never put me in harm's way or give me away to any stranger. That's why we live so far away from everyone else, so that no one could take me away.

As I got older, he would allow me to do more stuff. Sometimes his back would hurt, so I helped him take the big sacks downstairs. I learned that inside those sacks were bodies of people, voices, that he had stopped from getting in here. He told me that those bodies were filled with organs that people wanted so badly to live. He told me that the men who constantly showed up every week would come here and pick them up to sell elsewhere. I learned that some of those bodies were misplaced women. Prostitutes! They would get in his truck for money, expecting a good time, so he brought them home to keep us safe and sell their bits!

First, I was only allowed to lift heavy things for papa, like the big sacks and his tool bag. Then he would let me come down in the basement with him and put the bodies on the table. Papa had all the neatest things down there. He had a sink that brought water into the house, fresh clean water. We had a sink in the bathroom, but it did not bring water no matter how many times you turned the knob. It was frustrating. I was able to wash my face and take a drink without going to the creek in the back yard. In the wintertime, I no longer had to melt snow to get fresh water to bathe or drink. It was life changing!

My first task for papa was to help him hold the bodies open to retrieve the organs. Papa would use a little hand saw to cut the bodies from the throat all the way down to their belly button, and he had a few pieces of metal that would hold them open, but sometimes they were just too small to hold together, especially when he brought home bigger bodies like drunk businessman and even a high school boy that he found in a river, at least that's where papa said he found him - he was soaking wet after all!

I would sit on the table, on the person's chest or legs, and hold them open while papa got their organs. He would teach me the name for each individual organ - heart, lung, kidney, liver, eyeball, stomach, intestine, all of it! People had one of some and some of one and it was all interesting to learn. I was always excited when he brought a new sack home to see what it would be, and what I would learn next.

Once I learned where everything was, papa showed me how to remove the organs out, he allowed me to help him take them out. Soon, I was as good as papa, pulling out bits and placing them into special bags on ice. I remember one day I had a heart, both eyeballs, a liver and two kidneys removed for an order papa had in less than an hour. They were packed, labeled and dated for the delivery to be made and he even said that my work looked better than his! He was pleased with my work. I couldn't remember a day that I felt such joy and accomplishment, I always worked so hard from that day on.

As papa aged, I took on more and more of his responsibilities in the basement. No longer did I have to hide in the closet when he brought sacks home, I was eager to get started every single time. He said that I helped him out so much, he would have to find more and more bodies to bring home. Eventually he traveled further to find more bodies; at times I was left at home alone for days without knowing his whereabouts, that frightened me the most.

My 18th birthday finally came, an age I was looking forward to for so long. I was finally an adult, and this meant that now I will be given more task for this family business. I was so excited to celebrate, so happy, but it turned out to be the saddest day of my life. Papa had been promising me for weeks that he would make me my first birthday cake, but when the day finally came, he said we were out of 'milk'. He said that his back was hurting him too much - in his age he had many back pains, he was always uncomfortable and said he couldn't do many things because of it, but he promised me, and this was something I was expecting for a very long time... For the first time in my life I was mad at papa... This anger is what turned my life into a living nightmare. In my rage, I took a change jar papa had given me, and I told him I was going by myself to get some milk from the local store. There was actually a grocery store 30 minutes down the road. Papa attempted to stop me from leaving the house, but he was too weak and in too much pain to catch me. I left alone.

The walk was long, I should've cleared my head, but I didn't. I was still angry until I saw the grocery store, filled with magical lights all over. I stood in front of the door, and for the first time in my life, I saw my reflection, I saw my own face in the glass. I stood, staring at the young girl who was looking directly at me. She had wavy brown hair all the way down to her hips, I had green eyes and freckles all across my cheeks. I had a dimple on my left cheek when I smiled, and the wider my smile got, the more my dimples came out. I couldn't imagine that I had a way to look.

I opened the squeaky glass door and went over to the milk. I looked the milk carton over, there were so many colors and pictures, things I had never seen. I looked at the other snacks too, I had seen some - what papa bought for me. They even had fresh fruits up on the counter - bananas? I had never seen one of those before. I even bought one just to try it.

When I went to pay, I put the change jar that I had taken from papa on the counter and the boy across the register took the milk and counted out the coins. While he was tipping the coins from the jar, I saw him looking at something on the milk. I had no idea what he was looking at. He pointed to the milk and said that I look just like the girl on the side of the carton. I thought he was silly, so

I took it up in my hands, and checked it out. There, for the love of God, I saw myself staring back at me, alongside a picture of a little girl that was supposed to be missing. The boy said that he would feel more comfortable if I waited there, and we stared at each other for some time. His hand kept slipping below the counter, I could hear a frantic click. I wondered if this was normal. Why did the milk carton have my face on it?

After a couple of minutes, big trucks with red and blue flashing lights showed up, it was so loud and scary I had never heard anything like that before. These men in suits shoved their way into the glass doors, and had guns drawn. The boy told them that I was the girl on the milk, and even showed them. One of the men in armor came over and took my arm, he asked me my name, but I said I didn't have one. They grabbed me and threw me into the truck and said that they were the police. I was taken into a little building and they made me tell them everything I knew, so I did. I told them about papa, about the rats, about the closet, about the basement and papa's work. I told them where we lived, and a few of the men ran off in that direction, out of the building. They told me that I would sleep there for the night, so I slept in the cold hard jail cell, on a bed made of cement and sheets. I heard many sirens; many alarms and more men left the building. That night, they told me that they would finally "bring him to justice for what he has done to me". I was so angry.

They took papa. They took him, and they killed him at the house. He refused to come alive, so they shot him 12 times with their guns. They raided the house and told me that I belonged to two other people and that they were my mother and my father. I was placed in their home and was told they would take good care of me, but they were not papa. I was now alone, and they destroyed him, but in my resentment, I will keep on with my family business. My 'parents' gave me this journal, and if you are reading this you are reading my business log, as I stare at my parents hanging upside down with ropes clutched to their ankles and all their guts sticking out. Papa would be so proud!

Dream Letter 7

It was all in the Circumstances

Mom and I were on a trip to the islands - she was a nurse with a mission group, sent to help those recover from violent storms in third world countries. We got on this massive ship with everyone else to prepare for the month-long adventure. She was allowed to bring me only because she was a single mother. It was so cool being able to travel with her. I had never been on a ship before. While she was away in training, I was allowed to roam the ship and do whatever I wanted. I think I ate more soft serve ice cream than any other kid that year. It was great, an unforgettable adventure.

One day, we were warned that there would be a large storm coming, they advised us to pick up food for the evening since everything was going to be closed until further notice. I had squirreled away a large pizza pie, tons of tapioca pudding from the buffet, and a few apples to pretend like I was being healthy. Mom didn't come to our room, her training was running longer than usual, so I stuck it out alone that night with my Nintendo Switch.

The seas became more and more rough, and soon there was a special light above the door of my room flickering on and off. I felt the nervousness sneaking up in my throat as I watched the bookcase rock back and forth.

Soon, warnings were issued, and I could hear rain and waves beating off the side of the ship. We rocked around, all that pizza I ate was about to come out of my mouth in vomit. The captain put out a hurricane warning and everyone was ordered to come to the auditorium to collect life jackets and stay in just in case we needed to evacuate.

I sprinted out of my cabin, trying to find the big auditorium; I broke through the crowd to the upper deck. The rain was beating down, so severely that it stung my skin. I called out for my mom, trying to look for her in the rushing crowd, but I couldn't see her familiar face. I continued through the mass of people into the auditorium. Before the door could close behind me, I heard my name and saw my mom in a sea of people trying to get to the life jackets. I tried to move back against the current of people to get to her, but I froze when I saw the largest wave, yet come up, towering over our ship. In that wave were a group of whales, overhead, soaring through the sky in the turbulent water. As quickly as it formed, the wave washed over the ship, and the massive mammals smashed into the ship.

The sound was deafening, the animals screamed in a melodic horror show, and they ripped the ship apart. At least two landed directly onto the ship itself, while multiple others were thrown into the side, tipping the ship past its safety level and soon, the ocean became the sky. Everyone on the deck who had not yet been in the auditorium was thrown from the ship into the blood-filled water - the two whales who crushed the top part of the ship were ripped apart, shredded by the structure of it. Their blood stained the water and warmed it as it leaked around us. I plunged into the raging sea. I lost track of my mother, and almost of the surface before I was able to take another breath.

A shrieking yelp emerges as I filled my lungs with air, the taste of salt, iron and minerals filling my mouth, nostrils and eyes as I tried to find something to get on top of. I splashed and clawed for anything, screaming for help, but all I grabbed was air and more water. At one point I grabbed a person floating on the surface, I pushed him away from me as I noticed that he was no longer living.

After what felt like an eternity, I felt a hand grab the back of my neck, pulling me out of the water by my shirt with a sound of effort and some tearing of cloth. I grasped and screamed, trying to take in as much air as possible, and coughing up all the water that had invaded my lungs. I tore at my face to try and rub the sea water out of my mouth. When I was able to see, I found myself on a boat with six other people. A man had pulled me into the boat with one of his massive arms - was he a sailor? Where had he come from? I had never seen him on the ship before.

The other people were passengers I had seen during my mother's mission training. There was a middle eastern couple, an elderly woman, a little boy, and a middle-aged woman. They were all shaking, and some were huddling together. The little boy clung to the leg of the older woman. No one spoke, but we drifted farther and farther away from the ship as the storm cleared itself. We saw people sitting on the back of the floating whale corpses for moments, quietly catching their breath until the bodies of the whales began to sink.

Come the next day, we were all exhausted. The little boy had been sleeping for hours without moving, and the old woman had him curled up in her lap. We had been exposed for 12 hours, the sun was fully up and with the moisture on our skin - we were roasted alive like basted chickens in an oven. The salt burned as well. By the end of the afternoon of the first day, the boy wouldn't stop crying. His skin was blistered and raw, weeping. The Arabic man's head was as red as a tomato and some of the flesh were turning black from the extent of the burn. We craved water, and our stomachs roared. Nighttime was welcome - it was cool, the sun was gone, and we were alone in the world. At least the stars could see us. Would we ever be found? That was the argument going back and forth.

The next morning approached, my lips were blistered and peeling. My lips were so chapped I couldn't talk or lick them because I feared that more skin would peel off. The old woman looked the worst out of all of us. She developed oozing sores on her face, and eventually lost consciousness in the evening heat. She woke up a few times, but when her seizures began, we knew she wouldn't wake up after that. With a bit of respect, we slid her over the edge of the boat - and I could have sworn I saw a tentacle reach up from the bottom of the sea to grab her.

The water looked so gloriously blue in the purple and pink sunset, as if I was staring into another galaxy. The longer I stared, the more tentacles I saw lashing around just under the surface of the waves. They licked and lolled over the body of the old woman, dragging her down, deeper and deeper like soft arms bringing her into a hug. Soon, the body was out of sight, but I could also see other things that were not tentacles moving deep under the surface. I stared and stared, I squinted into the deep to try and see what else was moving down there, and after a moment - I was almost scared out of my sin as a dorsal fin of a shark clipped the very tip of my nose.

As the sun went down, and some of us snapped out of delirium, we noticed there were sharks all around us. We stayed in silence hoping they would swim away.

We saw many fish just under the surface of the water, ripping everything around us apart. They looked like scales of the sea, glistening in the water. Darkness absorbed them and we prayed that they wouldn't think our boat was something to eat alongside everything else.

The morning rushed, and the middle eastern woman was also unconscious from lack of water. Her husband would coax her awake, but she barely responded. Once the sun was high in the sky, her delirium drove her to drink seawater. She guzzled it down, drinking an entire belly full of seawater. She said how satisfied she felt and encouraged us all to do the same. The mysterious man at the end of the boat told her that she just killed herself and didn't even know it.

She kept screaming at us to drink the water, she scooped a handful of it and placed it against the child's face. He kept his lips pursed tightly to not let any in his mouth. To appease his wife, the man dipped a hand down into the water and drank it as well - he acted as if he was about to spit it out due to the salt and poison in the water, but he hung onto it. He let it roll in his mouth over his tongue and we could see him think about it. He reached his hand down into the water, and brought up another cup, he drank it and proclaimed how sweet it seemed.

They kept pressuring us to drink the seawater with them to save our lives. The mysterious man at the end of the boat advised me to ignore them, that the salt took over their minds and that I was better off sticking my ground. My stomach growled violently.

Over the course of the day, their seasickness became so severe. They threw up all of the water they had consumed, until they were vomiting blood. They continued to vomit, and their skin sweat heavily. They curled onto the bottom of the boat and shivered, the salt destroying their muscles from the inside. They held their stomachs and I could see their cheeks turning red as their fevers climbed even higher. They eventually succumbed to seawater poisoning and lay as crumpled balls of people on the bottom of the boat.

The boy, the man and I sat on the other end of the boat watching their bodies decay in the sunlight. Our stomachs were so empty we could barely think. I could have sworn I saw a ship, I screamed to my partners, pointing at the massive white object in which I thought it was another rescue boat, coming to sweep us off the water, coming to give us something to drink and a lovely sandwich to fill our bellies, but the man shook my shoulder, and told me to blink. I did, I listened to him and I wish I never did. The boat was a cloud high in the sky, I had been pointing up the entire time. It disintegrated in the wind as quickly as it had formed. I felt crushed. My stomach was made of venom, consuming me from the inside out. I held it but it roared within me, and the boy began to cry about his hunger as well. His skin was so raw and bloodied, he looked like a piece of meat himself, and he cried and cried, his little hands reaching for anything to eat, but only finding empty air.

That night, in the cool reprieve of darkness, the man finally moved from his spot. He went over to the couple laying, stiff, in the bottom of the boat and took out a flip knife that was stuck into his pocket. We heard him making a lot of noise in the darkness, but there was no moon to show us what he was doing. This was probably for the best. I am thankful that I never had to see his actions. He came back to the both of us with something in his hand, something moist and soft and sweet smelling. He told us to eat it, and to keep ourselves facing his way in the morning, so we wouldn't have to see his work. We ate what he gave us. It was chewy and fatty. It had the same irony taste as the water when the whales bled but amplified a thousand times.

Every bite brought more of the sweet metallic flavor into my mouth and I couldn't resist eating more and more of it. It not only quenched my thirst but filled my stomach and I enjoyed it so much. I asked for seconds as the night went on, and the man obliged, returning from behind us with more food, and we ate more of it. The little boy became full and rested his burnt body on the bottom of the boat. Morning came sooner than I had hoped, I wished it to never come not only to save us from the sun, but from the horror that sat behind us on the boat.

The little boy was whimpering in his sleep due to the pain of his flesh in the morning sun. We could almost hear the sizzle of his sores that had begun to fester and pus.

I had asked the man what his purpose on the ship was - I had never seen him in the mission training sessions. The man told me that he was being transported to the country for special holding for things he had done back home. He was being sentenced to life of hard labor to correct and atone for his mistakes. I asked him what he had done, and he said the same thing that was currently saving our lives today. He said that crimes were only crimes in the circumstances they were committed. He showed no remorse.

That next morning, we screamed in joy as we saw an island on the horizon. At first, I saw it, behind the man in the distance, ever so slowly coming closer, and I thought I was hallucinating again, but it never went away. Finally, I told him to turn around and look and he did. He also screamed in joy. The boy didn't say anything. His sepsis was flowing through his veins and infecting his brain, lungs and organs. He lay in shock on the floor of the boat. As we neared the island, we could even see buildings on it. How incredible I thought, that we landed somewhere so safe.

After a few hours the boat came ashore on a white sandy beach. I jumped off the boat, grabbing onto the sand with both of my hands. We looked around, I turned my back on him as someone neared us asked me who I was and how I had gotten there, and I told them. They were surprised I had drifted so far, but this was the island I was intended to land on. I asked them to help the boy in the boat and the man too, but they said that there was no one behind me. We went to look, and only saw a boat filled with bodies, including that of the man who was not suffering any issues when I was talking to him a moment ago, his skin wasn't even red from the sun. The man and woman's bodies were destroyed from our consumption, but his hands and clothing were not bloody. The little boy lay rancid and dead, as if he had been steaming in the sun for days. He also had no blood on his hands or around his mouth. The authorities did not question me, they only took me to a room to wash up and they even called a doctor over to help me heal.

After a couple of glasses of cold brisk water and a lengthy amount of rest, I began to remember what happened. I was in the boat all alone when the ship crashed, with no more supplies of food or water, I drank the seawater, causing me to hallucinate, and as the boat that I was in drifted to sea, I found dead bodies floating in the ocean in which I pulled onto the boat for comfort. I was the one who feasted on them! I feel so terrible for my sins but as I looked into the mirror, I whispered to myself, "it was all in the circumstances", and I never looked behind me again to see the terrible things that laid there.

Dream Letter 8
What I Will Do for Love

When I think about love, I think about red roses, long white veils, my prince charming standing in the alter as I am walked down by my father. That would be consider the American Culture wedding, in my case, the groom breaks a glass at the end, and we call it happily ever after. My mother urged for me to find a Jewish man to marry, she calls it formal, but I disagree. It feels like a blind date every time a new visitor comes to the house. My stomach cringes every time I stare into their eyes. I make them nervous and at times word vomit flows out of their mouth uncontrollably. Maybe I don't fit in, into their custom norm. Mother tells me it's a sin in Gods eyes if we do not obey His rules and apart of His rules is to marry a man and flourish my womb with lots of children. I was eighteen years old at the time and not once have I ever had a man lay hands on me or even give me a kiss on my lips. How would I ever be ready for marriage. Sounds insane to marry a man because of your religion, how is that love? I guess as a Jewish woman I am not entitle to much but to obey a man who self-claims to love me.

My life was ruined the day I turned eighteen, my father told me that he had found a husband for me. I laughed at his comment and figured he was just being a silly old dad. He slapped me across the face and told me to leave humor behind with my childhood, he claimed that I was a woman and I should start acting like one. Life is not for laughter but for work and family. He had found a new family for me to go to. I lashed out on him on how he could do that to me, how he could arrange my marriage like this. My mother had no words to offer, she encouraged my father's decision as the submissive wife that she was.

My marriage was arranged to some old man that bought me, some 44-year-old who was overweight and had a bald spot on his head. Some old man who stunk like cigars and beer and wore too many gold rings. On our wedding day I was asked to dress modestly, conservatively, and not wear much makeup. He wanted me to look as youthful as possible, he didn't want a slut to take home on the first night. He wreaked of cologne and was drunk the entire ceremony. When I had a minute to break free from his side, I went to my father and asked him why I had to stay with this man. My father told me that the man had a lot of money, I would be safe and secure with him for the rest of my life, he insisted he was an adequate person. Truthfully, at the time, he did seem pleasant. He was very charismatic to everyone at the ceremony and he had won my father over which is hard to do. I nodded that night and told my father that I would trust his judgement if this was the fate that I must have.

My wedding night was terrible. I was beaten, thrown against the wall. My young, preserved body was ripped to shreds under this man's enormous weight on top of me. No matter how much I screamed or how much I bled he told me that this was my job to him, and that I owed him for the nice life he has given me. What life was I being given?

He struck me across the face when I didn't move the way he wanted me to. Same night of our wedding, he struck me in the eye with his fist because I didn't move my hips enough. I learned a lot that night. I can still feel the soreness of the bruises and mutilation.

I tried to tell my mother a week later when he allowed me to leave the house, and she had no idea what I was talking about. My husband told my mother that we were both so in love and that I did not want to spend any time apart from him - that's why I hadn't visited them. This was my first time away from my family and she thought I wouldn't want to see her? My mother was my rock. I didn't talk to my father that day. No one I confined in believed me when I told them about the abuse I was going through. He was so wealthy, so kind, so generous, how could he be so abusive? Everyone assumed I must have been too greedy or selfish to make such accusation. I promise you; I was not.

The abuse continued for a year, and within that year he began to insult me, telling me how terrible I was at sex and that I was a whore for not giving him a baby. I had no idea what he was talking about, it wasn't like I was doing anything differently. I wasn't fully sure of the process - we were conservative Jews, the topic about sex was never allowed at home. He continued to use my body, however, and beat me whenever he thought about the fact that I wasn't pregnant yet. This continued for some months until I got a call from my mother.

Mother told me that my father and his other substantial members in the Jewish community were attacked in their meeting. A Nazi broke into their rented conference meeting and shot fire to everyone who were there, only some made it out alive. The police told her that the terrorist had fired over a hundred rounds in the building. She was in tears and my heart sunk. My husband, who was always looming over my shoulder when I took phone calls, took the phone from me and wished my sobbing mother as much wellness as she could get, whatever she needed, he would provide. He was her son in law after all. I heard her sing him graces on the other end, they discussed funeral costs, and he said it wasn't anything she had to consider. She thanked him again, and they ended the call. My heart was empty. My father had been killed in a hate crime and my husband seemed as if he could buy away my mother's pain.

Time passed and I cried every night after my husband fell asleep. I cried for my dead father, and my only hope of leaving this terrible marriage. I cried for my own body and how it was being torn apart day after day with barely any time to heal in between. I was crying because I felt trapped… I didn't know what to do, I was panicking in my own bed, lying next to the man who wanted to make my life a living hell. No one seemed to listen to me, not even my friends. I felt alone.

Finally, after one night of a particularly brutal beating, I worked up the courage to unlock the bedroom window, and with some fear in my heart and knowing that landing three stories to my death was better than living how I was, I snuck out to the tree limb just outside the window. I was covered in bruises from what that terrible man had done to me, my legs were quivering due to the pain in my muscles radiating down to my feet, I could barely climb the limb, let alone stand properly. To prevent myself from falling, I gripped onto the limb so tightly my hands became sore. I was so scared, clinging to that tree branch, I almost considered going back inside. How bad could the beatings be? Worse than falling out of that tree? I guess at the time I didn't think so, I shimmied myself the entire way down. A half an hour later, my inner thighs were rubbed raw and bloody from the bark, and the same with my hands.

At last, I was free, with nothing to my name but myself. I had no idea where to go, so I returned to my mother's house. I knocked on the door to no answer, the moon was just beginning to set, the hour of the night must have been strange, but still I knocked. Finally, when she dragged herself out of bed to the door, she seemed absolutely horrified to see me standing there, blood dripping from my nightgown between my legs were the flesh was torn away from the bone. I held out my hands so she can see, my bloody raw palms, raising them high towards the sky as I pleaded for help, I told her everything that happened, as I fell on my knees outside of her porch. I cried my soul to her to let me in, to give me somewhere safe to live.

She shooed me away like a stray dog begging for food. She told me to leave her porch and head back home to my family where I belong. She said that I must be the problem if I was running away and climbing trees, it was my job to serve my husband in any way he wanted, regardless of the circumstance - she said he didn't seem so bad, he was always generous in the community. My eyes were filled with tears of hate, scorn and fear, and I ran from her. I ran, in my nightgown in the middle of the night, with tears falling effortlessly from my eyes, blurring out the lights in the city. Finally, I ran so far that my feet started to bleed after I ran over some debris on the sidewalk, I had to stop and sit on a park bench.

I sat and sobbed into the silvery light of the morning. I sobbed to the ducks in the pond in front of me, they really didn't seem to care, they continued being ducks on a pond. The sun was beginning to rise, and I heard people walking down the road behind me to their jobs for the day. I didn't care what they must've thought of me, I was so broken and alone. After a moment, I felt like someone was staring at me, so I looked over my shoulder at a man in a white-collar outfit who was holding a briefcase and his jacket in his elbow. He asked me what was wrong, why I was in the park all alone in my pajamas, he asked me why there was blood pouring out of my hands, legs and feet, and he asked me why I was so emotional.

I couldn't resist pouring my life onto this man, this stranger in the park who was only on his way to work. I couldn't help divulging all of my story to him, I wasn't ashamed of it. He didn't say anything, he just let me talk to him. It was nice, finally having someone to listen to me, someone who would hear. I showed him my hands, and he looked at my feet, and when he sat down next to me on the bench, I thought he was going to say something, but instead he took his shoes off, and placed them on my swollen and sore feet. He told me that I couldn't walk bare footed anymore, the city wouldn't like my bloody prints all over the sidewalks. He gave me a wink and told me that I was welcome to come home with him and use it to put myself back together while he worked, so long as I didn't steal anything from him. I agreed, I wasn't a thief, and I did need to clean myself up. I asked for his name, he stared into my eyes and said "Elias".

His home was an apartment on the third floor of another building just around the corner of the park. He helped me walk up to the apartment, and I didn't have to touch a single thing, he walked me into the bathroom and turned on the warm water. He put soap in my hands and told me to clean my wounds, and when I was finished, he wrapped my hands gently with a long cloth band aid on each hand. He said that now I could use my hands safely, and I was free to be on my own, I could leave whenever I liked, he just asked that I locked the door once I was ready to leave.

I cleaned myself up the best I could, I put on some old men's slacks and a button down to replace my bloodied and tattered nightgown. I brushed my hair and made it into a long braid that swung down to my hips, and I kept a pair of his socks on my feet to protect my injuries. I felt much better, I was refreshed, and I felt as if I was given a chance to get my feet under myself, gain some composure and grow a tad.

Elias came home, I stayed to greet him and prepared him a home cooked meal while he was away at work. We got to talking, and we decided that I could stay in his apartment as long as I liked. We talked quite a bit over those next few days, he even took me shopping at a local women's shop to restock my closet in his spare bedroom. I had never seen my husband again, and eventually filed for divorce without contact.

A few months had passed, and I was feeling a little strange, I was falling in love with this man. The craziest part about it all is that he is a German, and my family will never approve. He was good to me though. I felt love, I felt happiness in my heart. We did everything and anything together. When we made love, it felt like actual love. Not force, but love.

After a couple of weeks, I started to feel nauseous and a bit lightheaded. Elias insisted that I should take a pregnancy test, in which I did. As I patiently waited for the results, Elias grabbed my hand and kissed it over and over again ensuring that he will bring joy and happiness to our new life despite of the criticism of others. I smiled back at him as I saw the results on the pregnancy test. "Positive". I jumped on him as he hugged me tightly. I felt safe, I felt protected. This is what I've been waiting for all my life.

Until the day were my sadness creeped again, I saw Elias sitting on the couch, with a letter on his hand. He told me to sit right across from him, it was important, he needed my undivided attention. He stuttered a couple of times, wondering his eyes elsewhere. Sweat was dripping from his forehead like a leaking faucet. I asked him what was in the letter. He stayed quiet. I yanked the letter from him and noticed a court date on it. I laughed and told him If he had gotten some sort of a parking ticket, he encouraged me to keep on reading. I did as I was told to only understand that his father was the man responsible for shooting and killing my father.

I lashed out in anger and yelled at him for not telling me the truth. He insisted that he was only doing it for my own protection, he didn't want to see me hurt. He wanted me to live a better life; he was willing to take full responsibility for his father's action. He had to testify because he was a prime witness but all he cared about was helping his father and ensuring that he only got minimal time for his crime. I was disgusted to hear this. I ran into the bedroom, filled up by backpack with some clothes and ran away not looking back. All I heard was Elias shouting, begging me to return back to him.

Racing through the New York City streets, I prayed for a car to hit me and kill me instantly.

Now I write this letter to my future baby boy who I carry, I want you to know that I will always love you, despite of your family tree. I will always care for you, because no one cared for me. I will always protect you and keep you safe. You are my universe, and in that universe, you bring me peace. You will one day read this letter when you are old enough to understand. Moving to the United Kingdom has been the best decision for us, no one can hurt us, no one can judge us. Please don't hate me, I don't want you to know right now what your true blood is made of.

Dream Letter 9
Mother Forgive Me

I am sorry mother, for the way that I was when I was younger.

I remember how terrible I was to you while growing up. I know that I fought a lot. I can still remember when I knocked out one of my classmates, he fell off the jungle-gym and had to get six stitches in the back of his head… His mother got a lawyer and you had to spend a lot of money fixing up the damages that I had caused. My heart is destroyed knowing that I was once that child, a miserable, ungrateful child.

Back in elementary school when I started smoking, it broke your heart to see me partaking in something so dangerous to my health. I do remember loving them at first, it really helped to pull me back down to earth, ease the anxiety I had stirring in my heart - without realizing it was breaking yours. You tried to get me to stop, but instead I stepped on your foot, broke the urn with grandpa's ashes in it, and ran out of the house for a week. You were only trying to do what was best for me at the time, I was just too stupid to realize it. If only I had the chance to go back in time and change everything again. Remember the promise ring I got you for Mother's Day? I promised to behave and be a better son. I continuously failed over and over again. Dad not being around was tough and you still managed to take both roles, raising me the best way that you could. I hate this feeling of guilt.

The first time I tried heroin was in my Junior year of High School. I needed to be more of a threat. I was so concerned with drinking, partying, getting laid and chasing girls that I needed something to take me to the next level so I wouldn't get stale in my position. I didn't want anyone to think I was getting boring, I wanted to be respected even more. It was expensive, and you noticed the rent money was missing. You had to pull a double shift that week to cover the missing money so we wouldn't get evicted. I didn't realize how much of a struggle that was at the time because I was too busy getting high. I would rip the house apart in parties that I would host to later understand that none of my friends had any respect towards you. Mom please forgive me.

I still can't believe I got arrested in High School. Me and some girl were having a great time after class at the top of the logging road - well, I was having a great time. She was just there for the drugs. The landowner called the cops, and we were so surprised to notice both cops standing outside of my vehicle while we were having sex. The cop forced me out of my car and practically nailed me to the ground. My needles and my baggies fell out with me. They put me away so quick - I had so much on me. They felt like they were bringing down some kingpin when in reality they were locking up a kid who barely had any sense in him. I am sorry for the money you lost in order to bail me out. I feel disgusted with myself to realize that not a "Thank You Mom" was given when you got me out of jail. I am sorry for the fights I caused because I was too busy getting myself into gang violence rather than going to Church with you. I cannot apologize enough.

Friday night came by surprise, in all the worst ways. We were fighting about rehab - I was dead set on not going. Why would I change? I was making money, getting girls, no one talked down to me - no one but you. I couldn't stand it. You saw me as some diseased animal, something that needed treatment to get whatever was wrong with it, cured. You made me feel like a victim when in reality I was only doing it all to myself - I just didn't know it yet. I remember that day I hit my peak when my hand ran across your face, I still remember the sharp clap my boney hand made against your skin. That sound now accompanies the sound of my heart shattering every time I think of that night. Putting my hands on you has been my biggest regret yet. Watching you sit on the floor in astonishment made me feel powerful, it made me feel strong, it made me feel like I was right in what I did. I had no foresight. I had no hindsight. I just didn't have my eyes open at all. I was a blind teenager running loose in the world wreaking as much havoc on myself and my loved ones. You were just trying to stop me from destroying myself, and yet I beat you.

That night I left angry, I wanted to be with my "friends" and forget about everything that was going on at home; I left into the rain without a coat. Your eyes were as wet as the sky as I turned from you. The sadden look in your face will never leave my memory. It was the last time I saw your eyes and they were crying because of me. Lord knows how much I wish that night never happened.

I headed over to Mike's house, in hopes to get high, we snorted cocaine for the first time, I was very lightheaded. I had a couple of chicks trying to sleep with me that night and in attempt to kiss one, my phone buzzed. I checked it out, it was some stupid Amber Alert, which I tried to swipe away but the EOS wouldn't let me, with no choice left, I opened it. I bolted upright as my fuzzy eyes, stilly hazy from the high, struggled to comprehend what I was reading...

"Black Kia Sorento struck head on by a tractor trailer who was unable to stop quickly enough in the rain - the Kia most likely didn't see it coming in the heavy fog. There were no survivors in the Kia, and the truck driver was badly wounded", were the words on the deep black screen imprinted on my phone.

I rushed out - I didn't have a car, so I ran the entire way home to you. The car wasn't in the driveway where you always left it. I slammed into the house - your keys and your purse were gone. On the kitchen table was a note you left me, "I am looking for you. If you are home, please stay here. I will be back". I felt my stomach in my throat as I crinkled the note and threw it at the wall, I ran back outside, in the drenching, pouring, bone-freezing rain and looked at the address where the accident took place. It was a really busy intersection just up the street, a little dip in town where fog always laid.

I ran so fast. My body was so worn out from all the garbage I had done to it, I could barely run to you. I was so worthless; I couldn't even make it to you without catching my breath once or twice. I ran until I felt a burn in my lungs, and then I would stand with my hands on my knees to catch my breath - and then I ran again. Finally, I came onto the scene, there was tape and police cars blocking off the entire intersection. The shipping truck was turned on its side, the upper door was pried off completely, the driver's section looked like an accordion.

I leapt over the cop cars and tape, the policemen were screaming at me to get back, but I wouldn't, I couldn't. I ran over to the car that was bent like a horseshoe, it was your car. I could see the bumper sticker "Proud Momma" still bright as day on the back. All the windows were shattered, and glass lay like snow on the pavement. The rain hit my face harder than ever and I ran to where you were laying, the cops grabbed me by my stomach and tried to pull me away, but I kept fighting them off. I yelled and screamed for forgiveness. Mom please come back to me, please don't leave me here alone, I am sorry. Sorry for being the worse son ever, I beg of you to come back to me. I blamed this on God, why would He take you away from me? Was this my lesson to learn, because I learned enough today. The cops were finally able to restrain me and sit me down by a near tree. The warm tears falling from my eyes only blurred the stretcher that was coming to lift you up, and as soon as I saw that the coast was clear, I ran up again to hold your hand one more time, in the midst of it, I slipped and fell face flat to the ground as your open eyes matched mines. I saw sadness in your eyes as I was once again carried away from the scene.

They placed me inside the ambulance with your dead broken body. You were shattered, just like I imagined your heart was from me. You were almost unidentifiable, but I could still see your soft face through the blood. I leaned on your body, and I cried onto you. I apologize way too late for my wrongdoings. I almost pushed you off of your metal bed.

What hurt me the most was to look at my phone and read a text that you sent me that said, "I forgive you son, I love you". This text could have been the reason for the accident. Hurts more to realize that you thought of me in your final moments of life.

As soon as I entered the house, I stepped on something, it was your promise ring I had given you - you always wore it even if your ring finger turned green. You said it gave you hope. I placed it in my pocket to keep it safe.

You were too broken and too destroyed for an open casket. Your funeral was quick. You had no family other than me. Some of your coworkers came, but they stayed only for a few minutes, said some kind words, and immediately left. I buried you in the dirt, so deep, where the sun would never get to you. I buried you, just like I tried to bury my own wrong doings - hide them so that it may never exist. I wanted to put this past me, but I couldn't. I can still hear your voice linger in my head, telling me how proud you are of me. Your soft-spoken voice telling me that no matter what, you will always be watching over me. Mom, I am sorry for all of this and I hope you can brighten me the opportunity to grow, to become someone in life, to become a man not a child.

I watched them put the dirt on your casket. It only took a little bit of time with the backhoe, and then you were gone forever as if you had never existed. The only proof the world had of you was me, and what had I done to show it? Killed you. God please have mercy on me.

I wear your ring every day now, as a promise to not only you, but to myself, and my family. My daughter looks just like you, you know? Same perfect skin, same glowing eyes, same softness in her soul. Are you in her? Are you helping to keep her safe? She is an angel, a blessing, just like you were, just like I failed to see. I named her after you just so you are close to me as I will always be close to her. I will teach her to not make the same mistakes in life as I did. I will give her love and patience just like you have done for me. I will not only ground her, but I will show her as well. I am leaving this note on your grave, because you are still with me every single day, and I cannot say these words enough to you.

Mom, I love you.

Dream Letter 10
Stay Here, Keep Safe

This house is cold and dirty, scary and lonely, and I hate it here.

I ended up here during one night when I pressured my friends into coming to this old abandoned, run down, filthy, empty house. The only thing accompanying this house were some broken furniture and cobwebs. The town wanted it demolished but it was a potential historical landmark, so it stayed in limbo. Some parties were held here, though they never turned out really well… This entire house killed the mood with whatever was happening in it. You walked in and suddenly your body felt heavy, the tension was at its peak. No one has lived in here in forever; even if you were alone, it always felt like someone was watching you.

We all came down here one Friday night, we were all exhausted from a long week of class and decided we should all have a drink. My girlfriend, Samantha convinced her brother to buy us a case of beer. This was the only house our parents will never suspect us to be in. We pushed open the door that had the fliers up "Do not enter". "Structure not safe for inhabitants". We didn't care we wanted to drink and enjoy each other's company. We got into the house, and the door led into the main room - it was a dark huge room, very dusty but we liked it here, no one was watching us now, no parents, just us or so we thought.

Victor tried setting the beer down in the front room and I whapped him over his head with my hand. How stupid did he have to be? What if some cop came by to check the place out and saw us drinking right here? What an idiot, so, I suggested we go downstairs to the basement. There, no one would hear us or see us or even rat on us. They tried to chicken out, but I insisted. I wanted Samantha to think I was brave, maybe she would like me more.

We went to the basement on my command. I felt like I was being pulled down there - maybe it was the hormone induced confidence? They all had to go down there with me, I kept getting angrier the longer it took for them to get down the stairs. What a bunch of pussies. When we went downstairs, we cleared off a place to sit in the dust covered floor and cracked open some cans. We talked and as we drank the bitter liquid, we loosened up a bit. It wasn't so bad down here. We used our cellphones as flashlights. It was just a cinderblock room.

Gretchen - a nerd - went over to some old bookcase that was anchored to the wall and thumbed through what was on it. I ignored her, I didn't have any time for books, what a waste. The rest of us continued talking ignoring her disappearance. We did always feel a little eerie, however. Mac commented on it, he felt like something was sitting next to him. Rose said she felt some kind of pressure pushing down on her.

Gretchen came over holding something stupid and she gave it to Victor. He said it looked like a board game - how dumb. Gretchen corrected him like she usually did with everybody and told him it was a Ouija board - you know one of those old ones that people played with before there was internet to keep them busy? Well, they all wanted to play with it. It was like some arcane relic, some spellbound mystery portal and we all huddled together. Gretchen even grabbed some old sconces from the walls upstairs and brought them down. Mac lit them with his lighter he stole to smoke when his mom wasn't home. I had to admit, with the board in front of us, the basement did seem spooky

We sat around this board, all of our fingers were on the keystone, and we asked it boring questions, well, the girls asked it questions.

Things started to get a little creepy. Rose asked it, what date it was? The keystone hadn't moved the entire time, but when she asked it again, we all felt a twitch. I don't know if my eyes were ever that wide before; Victor elbowed me and told me to quit screwing around. I told him I wasn't. They didn't believe me.

The key moved over the board, it twitched and turned and seemed to be pulled by everyone sitting in front of it, but all of our faces were filled with horror as we watched it. The key moved over some numbers that didn't really seem to make sense…. 92429. That wasn't a date? Right? It's 2020, I mean come on the least you could do was put something close to that in there, right? We all sat around this dumb board, as baffled as ever. Gretchen, the smartass that started this whole thing, took her hands off the key and held her face. She said she was too scared to continue, and the other girls agreed. Samantha was as white as a ghost; I could tell she wasn't feeling well so the rest of us decided that we would stop. It wasn't fun anyway. It was messing with my head and at that point I was too buzzed to continue.

We sat for a few minutes in complete silence, just staring at this board. How crazy was that. I wondered who had been the one to push the key around, everyone looked genuinely shocked. They were all doing a good charade.

Before long, something fell upstairs and made a massive clatter. The girls all screamed, and Rose demanded to leave. She wasn't having fun anymore and just wanted to go home, I think everyone was feeling that way at that point. We ran upstairs - leaving the beer and the board on the ground in an attempt to escape. When we all bumbled up the stairs, practically knocking the floorboards out of the steps, we saw what had made the massive crash. Pieces of floorboards upstairs had fallen down to block the front door and windows, like a massive tetanus infested fence. We were so stunned, we just stood with our mouths open looking at it.

Rose started crying - she was always the most sensitive one out of the three girls. Samantha tried to make her feel better and rubbed her back. Victor went over and tried to move the boards, but they were locked in together in the way that they fell, nails stuck out all over the board that made it too dangerous to touch them.

Mac said we could still climb out one of the side windows, he told us all not to freak out, and went over to the old window. He unlocked it; the lock was rusted shut so it snapped as he attempted to turn it. He was able to wiggle the piece out of the lock, and then tried to open the window completely, but it was so stuck in the frame that it wouldn't budge. It looked like someone had caulked it closed at one point, probably to prevent bugs and drafts. Victor tried to help him, and together they both couldn't open the window. They tried the rest of the windows on the first floor, and they all did the same thing. They were all bolted closed, caulked shut or frozen in the frame.

Rose didn't stop crying, Victor was visibly pissed. I would be too! I had no idea what was going on, but I tried to pick up one of the old wooden chairs to throw against the window, hoping I could break it, but when I picked it up, the back fell off of the seat and the wood fell apart in my hand. It was rotted out from all the years of just sitting here in the damp air. I dropped the soft wood onto the ground, and it made a dull thud against the floorboards. I was absolutely amazed and kicked the rest of the chair which just ended up falling apart into a pile. Mac picked up a leg which snapped in half and used it to beat one of the windows out. Rose cried harder than before. She kept repeating that we were trapped in here. Mac tried to help her feel better too.

Victor suggested going upstairs to try and open one of the windows to get onto the roof. Gretchen told him it was a bad idea, of course she would, because the floor just fell out from one side of a room upstairs. She did make a valid point. Victor and Gretchen started shouting at each other. He asked her if she wanted the whole second floor to fall in on us, and if that would make her happy. Mac told Victor to shut up, that he was making everything worse, and then those two got into some stupid fight about who was right. I had no idea. My head was so foggy – I was overwhelmed. I went over to the stairs to see what they looked like, wondering if they were even safe to walk on.

The stairs actually looked pretty decent in comparison to the rest of the house. Isn't there some saying that the last piece of a building that will remain will be the stairs because of the way they are built or something like that? Well, these ones looked pretty good to be honest. I figured I would go up alone, so that no one had to have an opinion about it. I took the first few steps slowly, and they creaked softly under me, but they didn't seem very scary.

Slowly I climbed up to the second story of the house, I felt more and more confident the higher I climbed, the stairs weren't bad at all. I could still hear them having a fight. I didn't want to put up with it. Upstairs, it was dark and drafty. The windows were broken out, one even had a limb of an old tree through it. I sighed thankfully, we weren't trapped in here after all, they were all just being a bunch of babies.

The broken window was placed in what turned out to be an old child's bedroom. There was peeling pink wallpaper glued up, but it was bleached by the sun over the decades. There were some pieces of furniture scattered around, a broken-down crib laid on its side since all the legs wore out from under it. Inside the crib laid a small photo frame; I went over to check it out. My curiosity just couldn't resist.

The frame contained, a super old photo of a baby in its communion gown, the white billowing, puffy cloth was surrounding it in the bed it was on. It was pretty grainy and hard to see, but it was definitely a baby. Was that the baby that lived here? When I lifted the frame higher in my hands to take a closer look at the picture, the frame broke apart, and the picture fell out, face down on the floorboards. I picked it up, and it said "Camelyne 1929" - 29? Wasn't that the last two numbers the board gave us downstairs? 92429.

I went back downstairs and saw the group sitting down on the floor, scathing at one another. I showed Mac the picture, and he agreed that was the same number given by the board. Gretchen determined that the Ouija board must have given us the date of September 24th, 1929, the baby looked to be a few months old, so it was most likely the date of the baby's communion... I was so caught up in that stupid old picture that I didn't notice Rose was gone. I couldn't hear her crying so I couldn't pin-point her. I asked the group, and no one noticed that she had gone anywhere. There was nowhere for her to go other than upstairs, or the basement, and she certainly didn't go there.

Victor and I offered to go upstairs again, maybe Rose had followed me upstairs or something, I probably didn't see her pass by while I was looking at the dumb baby picture. We went upstairs single file, the stairs creaked more with Victor on, of course it would with him being a 200-pound football player. He didn't seem to notice but he hung onto the railing, afraid the whole thing was going to fall apart. We walked by the room that I had been in – the baby crib was no longer there. The room was completely empty of furniture. He didn't believe me.

We went into the second room, what looked like a bedroom, across the hall from the baby's room. There was no one in here, we whispered for Rose, like we were trying to hide from someone else, hoping that she might appear out of the corner or something, but no. When Victor and I had our backs turned to the door, we heard her shrill, high pitched, and terrifying screaming coming from the room next door down the hall a little further. I ran out before Victor, and into the next room - an old bathroom, the tub filled with slime green water, and knives all over the floor. I looked around in there, but no one was in the room, just the gross tub. In attempt to exit the bathroom, I heard the drain of the tub gurgle; it made me look over. I stared into the deep green water, barely enough to see just below the surface, and I thought I was going to die when I saw Rose's face under the water. I reached in, trying to pull her up, the green slime sticking to my forearms, but every time I reached for her, she disappeared. When the water stilled and I could see into it again, her face reappeared, frozen in time with that same scream still on her face.

I ran downstairs and into the group, my arms all green from the algae upstairs; I asked them for help with the tub, but they were all shocked at my story and called me crazy. They asked where Victor was, I actually didn't know... He was in that other room with me, but didn't come when he heard me splashing in that tub - he had to have heard me right? I told them I was unsure... Now it was just Samantha, Gretchen, Mac and I.

I told them there was a window upstairs, in which we could get out of with a big tree limb through it, but none of them were comfortable enough to go up there.

While we were trying to figure out what to do, we heard Victor shout for help downstairs, in the basement where this had all started out. Mac told me to wait there, and that he and Gretchen would go check it out; Mac assumed the floor collapsed which led Victor straight into the basement. Although we never heard a crash. Samantha and I waited in the living room, sitting on the floor, by ourselves, while they disappeared into the dark basement again.

We waited for what seemed like forever, and finally Samantha told me she couldn't wait anymore, she had to go check on her friends. I figured that was the smartest thing to do, since no one had come back up or asked for help. What if Victor was really hurt? It wouldn't be possible for those two to carry him up all on their own. Samantha went first down the basement stairs; she used her cell phone to light the way.

I followed down behind her carefully. I didn't want to fall and take us both down with me. At the bottom of the stairs, in the giant open basement, there was nothing. The candles were still burning around the board, and the key was still in place, over the number "9" where we had left it. There were no signs of Victor, Mac or Gretchen; Where could they have gone, I thought. Samantha was standing next to me with her mouth agape.

She said we never said "goodbye" to the board. I had no idea we had to do that! She checked under the stairs for our friends, but no one was there... We were all alone, so we sat back down at the board, just us, with our fingers on the key.

She asked it where our friends were, and the key floated over some letters...

G O N E.

She asked them where they went.

H O M E.

She asked it what it meant.

L I K E M E.

One bookshelf wiggled gently against the wall, as if it was being pushed and pulled quickly back and forth, and only one book, that was tucked in the space where the board had been, flopped open onto the ground, spine up. Samantha went over to pick it up. When she flicked through the pages in the candlelight, she gasped and threw the book at the floor.

She said that it was a journal, from an old man who lived here. He didn't want the baby that had been delivered, and on its Christening day he tossed the baby in the basement, down the stairs, and locked the door. He said that his older son tried to protect the child, and in a brutal fight between the father and son, the father pushed his son out the window leading him straight to his death. In response to the mother losing both of her children and being married to such a monster of a man, she took the entire knife block to the bathroom and slit her wrists in a tub of water. He couldn't bear to stand his actions, so over the crumpled mess of the baby, he intended to hang himself in this basement.

We were both shocked. Samantha sat back down and placed her hand on the keystone. She asked who we were speaking to.

B O Y.

Which boy were we speaking to?

L I T T L E.

She asked if the board meant the baby. Had the baby grown up into a little boy in the basement?

Y E S.

Where was the rest of the family?

H E R E W I T H U S.

She asked where the brother was, and was he keeping him safe from all the bad things that was going on. "What was the brother's name?" she asked.

The keystone floated ominously around the board, moving quickly over a set of letters, but then the keystone turned, the point aimed at me, with nothing through the looking glass.

A L E X

When I looked up from the keystone, which was pointing ominously at me, I saw Samantha hanging from the biggest support beam in the ceiling of the basement. I couldn't believe it… I was in shock as I looked back at the board where the keystone was now moving all on its own.

S T A Y H E R E K E E P S A F E.

The basement door shut tight with a loud slam, and the candles were huffed out by an unsourced breeze. I write this now with the last light on my phone, using the blank pages of the man's journal, hoping that one day someone will find this and knock this damn house down, because if they don't, I will be trapped in here forever.

Dream Letter 11
Eliana

I woke up out of a dizzying haze, my head felt heavy. My mouth was dry, and my eyes burned. In an attempt to blink away the burn I clenched my eyes tightly and called out for my mother. There was no response. My vision returned. I tried to reach out to my mother whom was sitting in the driver's seat, however I realized my wrist were bound with a zip tie. I felt the pin pricks of pain in my chest. I saw that my ankles were also tied. I called again for mom and shook her shoulder harshly with my elbow, feeling my rage at her silence well within me. She did not answer but her head flopped to the side. It was only attached by a thin layer of tissue. Her throat was slashed so severely no bone held it up any longer. Her clothes were covered with blood dripping down from her neck. I screamed, an ear-splitting scream that filled the car as I pushed the lever of the old car door which seemed to open too effortlessly. I fell backwards onto the ground and looking up - a group of men in clown masks stood over me, laughing. One of them grabbed me by my hair and dragged me off into the woods.

I was dragged deep into the woods to a bonfire. The sun had just gone down, the sky was still purple, but I could see dozens of men around the campfire, in lewd poses and gesturing to me. I screamed even more, and one man raised a fist against my head hard enough to make my ears ring. I was barely able to hold my head up, but I heard them all chanting in a language that I could not understand… what was it? Latin? My head sunk and my chin hit my chest; I was unconscious again.

When I woke up the second time, I was in a granite cell with murky water pooling on the bottom. Iron bars were bolted into the stone to keep me inside. I could hear voices just beyond eyesight. I screamed for help again, shaking the bars with my hands. The metal was cool and rough to my damaged skin. I saw another group of these clown men approach. How long have I been in here? They entered my cell and one brought another fist down across the back of my head. They spoke to me with disgusting language, they brutally raped me to the point where my body bled. They made it very clear that they had other intentions rather than saving me. I was unable to resist as they grabbed ahold of my bindings. I lost control of my body in that cell.

I was thrown onto a wet mattress when they were done with me and I fell unconscious, the stress so severe I couldn't keep my eyes open any longer. In the dark pool of sleep, I felt my head rise from the surface, and then I felt a pain deep in my belly. Suddenly, I was on a silver exam table, a mirror at my feet and more clown men surrounding me. I could barely see the mirror over my enormous stomach. How could this be? It's only been a few moments? The pain forced me to close my eyes as I cried and screamed in agony. When I opened them again, a woman about my age and very similar features to myself was looking back at me. She wasn't me, so who was she? She was smiling at me, also pregnant. The pain washed over me in unrelenting waves before I could no longer tolerate it. I woke up from this dream with my used body still strapped to the soggy mattress.

A clown burst into the cell and ripped me from my feet by my hair. I was dragged into another room where another man waited for me with a hot cup of tea in the table. He asked me all kinds of questions about myself – "Do you know who you are?" Well, yes. Melody Hartford, recent graduate of Victoria Richmond University. He slapped me across the face for my answer. My lips split. He asked me where I was from, did I know my mother, did I know my father. I stayed silent if my answers were only going to be met with punishment.

The man accused me of being some demon, a succubus they have been waiting to return to them; to lift them into glorious pleasure. They were pleased that I had delivered myself so neatly to them just when they needed me the most. They wanted to free me from this treacherous "host". The interrogator blamed a woman named Eliana for the suffering I had been through. At this point, he was no longer talking to me anymore, but rather to something he thought was in me... a demon? A succubus? Perhaps that explains my vicious mood swings as a child, why I had to finish college from home, because I couldn't control myself at school. It all makes sense now, as to why I was so dangerous. Mother locked me in the house for my own protection, to prevent this demon from controlling my soul. A sharp hand across my face brought me back to the man's attention. I let my anger wash over me, and in a quick fit I tossed the hot tea onto the man's face. He screamed in agony as he attempted to swipe the scalding liquid from his eyes.

I aimed towards the exit door from the interrogation room, but something within me stopped me on my tracks. My legs remained stiff like concrete cylinders. My feet were glued to the floor and no matter how hard I tried to use them they wouldn't budge. They would not let me flee and find freedom. They would not let me go back to where my mother's body was. I stayed in that doorway until more clowns came at the call of the injured man, those clowns grabbed me under both arms and dragged me back outside, stating that this was needed to be done to free me from my mortal bindings. I was placed on a wooden slab on top of a star shaped altar. We were just beyond sight of the road and I could see cars passing by. I prayed for someone to rescue me, but each one continued driving away.

The clowns nearby touched themselves and each other in the most disgraceful of ways, they laughed and threw stones at me. My body was covered with dirt, grime and mud from the cell I was kept in. Their chanting only got louder to the point where I could no longer hear my prayers. They kept bringing up Eliana and how she will be counted as a sinner for the rest of her days.

Suddenly, a group of college boys veered down the dirt road and ran straight into the crowd, hitting some of the clowns directly. They yelled at them to let me go. One was wearing my school's jersey. They were here to save me! The clowns tried to grab them and hurt them, but one of the boys had a gun and shot a few rounds into the crowd. Some of the clowns were screaming in pain as they were severely injured by the bullets.

The clowns yelled back at the college boys, warning them that if I were to be untied, they will all be doomed in misery and regrets. One of the boys came over to untie me and placed me carefully in the back of his vehicle. They turned the car around, but the clowns were not surrendering just yet; they were trying to open my door but thankfully it was locked. As the college boys turned back onto the road, I could see my mother still sitting in the car that I had woken up in, her head still turned over unnaturally to the side, just hanging by a thread.

I laid in the hospital bed, my body was induced with more medication to prevent the countless amount of diseases and implications of the clown's actions on me. I was in so much pain - now that the shock was over, I could finally feel the wounds that were inflicted on me. My arms were broken in multiple places from being tied down. I had tears in my scalp from my hair being pulled on so roughly. I had countless bruises and scrapes all over my body. The nurse administered a couple of pain medicine that would help me sleep, and away I drifted.

In my drug induced sleep, I had such vivid flashbacks about how this all began... I persuaded my mother to allow us to go camping for the weekend out in the woods near where I was abducted. She allowed it, my behavior had gotten better and she preferred me to enjoy my youth rather than being locked up in the house.

I reached forward that day, to the driver's seat and sawed my mother's head almost clean off with a camping knife. I tied myself up, my ankles and wrists, so that I could not get away. I remember thinking "now I will be freed from this wretched soul". I laid in the car for hours before the clowns found me. I willingly did this all to myself.

Now, this woman in red scales looked at me, her leathery wings fanned out in irritation behind her. She told me that I had ruined her chance at freedom and independence and that I had taken her conquer of the world away from her. She hissed venomously at me. Her great onyx horns curled over her head. Admittedly she was beautiful, a body made for sex, but unfortunately, she was housed in my body. The demon woman gave me a run-down of who I actually was.

Eliana, the woman that these clowns had blamed so deeply for their disadvantage in whatever this hell cult was, was actually my mother. The woman that I had seen in the mirror on the first night of my abduction was surprisingly her. That is why her features seemed so similar to mines. My mother was brought into this cult, impregnated and was supposed to birth the demon that fueled these men's lust filled religion. They were dissatisfied to see that instead Eliana birthed a normal human baby. Eliana's throat was slit on the altar on which I was born, and I was thrown away into a pile of filth, only to be recovered at the scene by detectives and placed into the arms of my aunt, the woman who actually raised me. My mother's blood was used to attempt to summon the succubus again, but they were not aware that their conjuring created her within me, and within me she had grown and matured. She had gained strength from the men's actions upon my body although she always controlled a bit of me, no matter what. She made me rage when appropriate. She caused me to lash out as a child, but she most recently took control of my soul. Now she had every single intent of returning me to the altar where my mother died so that the same altar and chanting could be used to free her from my disgusting human form. She made sure to inform me that I would be destroyed in the process, and that I deserved it.

I know I need to die. Tonight, while my nurse is gone to refill my medicine, I will stand on the windowsill and jump. I just ask that whoever finds my body, please cremate it. I know the hospital has a crematorium in the basement. Please heed my warning. I cannot be as I am in death because that will never kill what is inside of me, just waiting to come out. Please burn me, so that you may burn her too and release her from our world, sending her back where she belongs - the deepest pit of hell. Please do this for me. I have no family. I have no burial request, just burn me and put my remains somewhere where they cannot be touched. I have not lived a good life, and I do not want to continue down the path she has paved for me. I hope whoever reads this understands, and I thank them for the fleeting kindness they have provided me in my life.

Dream Letter 12
I'll Do Anything to Save You

In this recap of my recent life, please know that I love my daughter, and I know that I did not make the right choice for her. I can only hope that when I rise to meet her that she will forgive me. I am trying to amend my poor decision and make right on the world for when I reach Heaven, I have no black mark on my record. I want my soul to be lightened of the burden I have been carrying, and I know that this is the right decision for me.

Olivia was such a bright light in my dark life. She was a result of a not-so-pleasant past, some people may even consider her to be a consequence of my actions when I was younger. I could never think that way of her, she was such a marvelous little girl, she was a reward, a blessing, a secret gift that only I was bestowed. I knew I was lucky the moment I laid eyes on her. She was a squirmy little thing who never wanted to sit still if only for a moment. When she was taken from me in the delivery room to run some tests and make sure she was healthy, I felt that the procedures were taking longer than normal. I waited and waited and still my baby didn't return. Finally, after nagging a nurse for some kind of information, the doctor returned to my room and told me that my beautiful little Olivia had a severe heart murmur, her heart valves were leaky meaning she wasn't pumping blood efficiently enough to support her tiny body. Due to her size and other complications, surgery wasn't an option so I was told to return home with her and savor our time while we could. We weren't given a timeframe of when to expect the worst, so every single day I worked hard to provide for her and give her the life I knew she deserved. I took on two jobs, during the day I worked at a hotel and at night I served tables at the local diner. They brought in meager earnings, but it was enough to pay the bills and even supplied me with insurance to get Olivia some medication to make her life a little easier.

She wasn't able to run around and play like the other children and was frequently tired, but she was the most beautiful thing I had ever laid eyes on while she slept. I loved her so fully, so completely, that I couldn't imagine life without her. I tried to demand doctors to take my heart to replace hers so that she could live to the fullest, but they refused to do it, saying that not only was it impossible on such a small child (my heart was too large and she would have other complications from that) but it was unethical. Euthanizing me to save my child was considered ridiculous and doctors wouldn't do it in an effort to preserve their license to operate. I was furious as I watched my baby decline. She became so tired and weak that she could no longer hold her own head up and eventually the seizures set in from lack of blood flow. They were so violent which rocked her entire little body, every time it happened I prayed and prayed that she would recover, or that God would make it stop, stop forcing my sweet little girl through such a terrible thing and take her to the Holy Land where she would be loved and comforted forever. He didn't take her before the strokes started.

When they came, they were also terrifying, and I hoped during each one that she would finally be taken from this hateful and cruel world but still she clung on. She was brain dead by the third, lost all motor functions and could only breathe on her own, and I laid next to her tiny failing body as I told her that she could leave, that she did not have to stay for me; I would be strong without her and see her very soon. I told her that she had to go and that she could no longer stay in this body as it was driving her away, and to take God's hand and leave to such a wonderful place. I feel that she had finally listened to me that time, as I could feel her tiny body take one last powerful breath. I laid my hand on her chest and felt her weak pulse grow smaller and smaller, I watched her tiny lips turn blue and the rosy pink in her cheeks flood away. I felt her chest fall still and soon her body stiffened as I laid next to her and cried. I could have saved her, my body was fine, and I could have prevented this from happening, but they stopped me. I was so angry and filled with hate, rage and sorrow that I did not move even when they came to take her away.

I must have laid there for days in her tiny girly bed. I did not eat or sleep or drink or move. I just laid there and stared at the ceiling. I thought of all the beauty that she put into my life, and all the glorious happiness she inflicted on me. I thought about how that was all taken away now. I felt the grief swarm over me like a cloud of poison. It entered every single cell I had and somehow felt like it filled me more than that. It caused my body to hurt and I felt my heart breaking - the heart that I intended to give to my daughter was now shattering in my chest and there was nothing I could do. I would die here too, from a broken heart, because I could not save my daughter.

Eventually I did get up, but when I did it was only to fetch a drink so powerful to help me wipe away the memories of her from my mind, but unfortunately nothing like that existed. I drank and drank until my money ran out, and then I had nowhere to go. I lost my home, I lost my love, and I lost my life. What would I do? I planned to drive to the ocean and throw myself into the waves and let it sweep me out so my spirit could be with her, so I took my car and my quarter tank of gas and tried to get as far as I could, but it was useless. I barely made it out of the state. In an effort to get more money to fill up my tank I took a job at a local diner. I had intended for it to only be for two weeks until my check came in, but I met a woman there who felt like saving me.

Her name was Rose, and she had a small daughter named Jody who was at home with an illness that prevented her from going to school. Rose saw how much my life lacked drive, so she let me confide in her with what had happened to my own little girl. Rose said that the diner was no place for me at the moment, and if I chose to, I could stay with her and live at her home and help her with Jody's care, as I was very experienced in the needs of special children. I wouldn't have to pay rent, and she would supply all my food and cover the utilities for the home. I took the offer, because I had nothing left at that point and the diner was crushing my soul. She asked me not to leave, and that she would value my help - what more could I say? Of course, I stayed.

Over the course of a few months I learned quite a bit about the family. Rose had suffered a violent divorce from her husband, Jody's father, because he could no longer tolerate caring for the girl. He hated both of them so much that he had to leave, and he took most of Rose's money with him, forcing her to get a job at the diner just to barely make ends meet. He didn't even leave her enough to provide a helper for Jody while she was away at work, so every shift was a risk for her. Rose had suffered a lot from the divorce, and she often cried in the kitchen late at night when Jody was in bed. She said it was just a way to release the stress but whatever she did she didn't feel any better. By helping her out with Jody, I was able to give her more time for herself while she recovered from her own depression. I was happy to have helped someone.

When I started living with Rose and Jody, I felt a bit like an outsider. I helped Jody dress and clean and eat just like I did with little Olivia. It was such a familiar task that the actions came to me with no effort. Jody was such a sweet little thing and she never complained about all of the extra steps I took with her to make sure that she was getting the best care. She seemed happy to have the extra attention and soon we formed a fast bond together.

Jody enjoyed story time, we re-read the same book until the pages began to fall out. She also loved to go on walks. She was getting stronger and stronger as she aged but for long walks in the fresh air and sunshine she needed to sit in a carriage, and I loved to take her out on walks all afternoon while her mother was working. She loved to watch the butterflies dance in nearby yards and flower gardens, and she pointed at clouds and talked about them regularly. She would bump around in her seat if she saw a dog or another walker. I still remember the time that she pet a man's little shih tzu - she was so amazed by the fluffy fur and the little cold nose that she squealed with glee. It was so heartwarming. I wondered if this is what Olivia would have been like if she had made it this far? She was more into talking and reading on her own than Jody, but that was ok. Every child is different, and they all require a little bit of effort in different things. I never compared the two critically to one another. That wouldn't have been fair. What they did have in common was their love of rainbows. Olivia always asked what was on the other side, and I gave her answers that she could find in all the story books, but she never sounded happy with any of them. Jody was the same way, and as much as it frustrated them it increased their ability to wonder.

I remember one day when Jody and I were out at the park. It was a little drizzly, so we waited under a pavilion to wait out the bit of rain since the clouds were moving quickly overhead. Finally, the rain stopped, and the sun burst out from behind the clouds; Jody stumbled out from the park bench she was climbing on and looked at the sky, pointing at the brightest most vibrant rainbow I had ever seen. We loved it so much and watched it for so long that it even developed a second fainter rainbow right overtops of itself. Jody was so thrilled while she watched this perfect rainbow pair that she didn't even realize the rain was laying in her hair.

Over the years Jody grew and grew and became healthier than ever, but one of the doctors told her mother that she had a heart murmur, the same condition that Olivia was born with, that had developed due to the delay in her earlier years. Her heart was struggling to keep up with the rest of her little body and they told Rose to fear the worst for her daughter. They said that she may live for some time, even into old age but she would have to be extremely careful of her activity levels and not to overwork herself. Overworking could simply be caused by walking up the stairs too many times. They also told her to expect her daughter to die early. They told her that there is a chance she could lose blood pressure resulting in a lack of flow to her brain, causing strokes and death, just like what happened to Olivia. I was not in the appointment with Rose, but I remember those words being spoken to me all those years ago and how I was devastated because of them. I remember the cutting pain they dug into me; I felt as if my daughter died that day as well when in reality it was the hopes and dreams, I had for her that died. I thought at the time that was just as painful, but it would be years until I learned the real lesson.

Jody still thrived for about a year. She still played at the park and enjoyed the sunshine and the rain and the snow and everything else that came with nature. She still walked around a bit, more or less shambling on tiny thin legs. She spoke well enough to tell us small stories and she even learned how to read, though she often kept that to herself as a quiet activity.

One day, however, Jody took a tumble when Rose had her out in the backyard playing with the dog. She tossed herself down the hill and it was all so quick… She tripped over untied shoelaces that I should have seen - I was her caretaker after all - but I did not notice them. I was too busy enjoying watching her and the puppy play in the warm summer afternoon. She screamed out, and it happened as if it was in a slow-motion movie. She tumbled head over heels, crashing into a pile of sticks and yard waste at the bottom of the hill. We stood, and could barely move, in shock. She was silent and both of us couldn't look away from her. Before I could regain myself, my feet were already in motion and I was running to her side. She laid unconscious in the brush pile and I screamed for Rose to call an ambulance and she did, I heard her on the phone with the operator who was giving her directions to stay calm.

I gingerly pulled Jody from the brush pile, picking off the sticker bushes and thorns from her clothing. Her skin was scratched to pieces from the twigs and spikes and vegetation that she fell into and she was covered in beads of blood from this. She was so silent, so still, but her eyes were fluttering every now and again and I recognized the symptoms of a small seizure. She tensed and relaxed over and over again, and I held her as her mother stayed on the phone with 911. It felt like an eternity before the first responders showed up, and they took Jody out of my arms and placed her on a stretcher with her arms tied down to her chest. They gave her a quick injection to stop the series of seizures she seemed to be stuck in. When she was in the back of the truck, she was given an oxygen mask and hooked up to so many monitors. Rose got in the ambulance with her daughter, and I was left behind in the yard with the dog while I watched the vehicle drive away with the loudest sirens and the brightest lights I had ever seen. Once Jody was out of view, I never stopped praying. I knew what I needed to do.

When I was allowed to visit, I went to the hospital immediately. Rose sat over Jody's bed and held her daughter's small hand in her own. She told me everything the doctors had seen on her screens and monitors. She continued to seize until the medicine kicked in. She seemed to go into a period of rest until she was admitted and given a bed in the hospital, where she immediately had a stroke. Her heart stopped, and they were very careful to do CPR and resuscitate her. Her heart did not want to start again because of its weak state to begin with. I felt myself nearly faint as Rose informed me of this. She said that Jody had lost the use of the right side of her body, but the only thing she had going for her was her age. Her brain may be able to heal enough to redevelop this portion, but her heart needed to be strong enough to get her to that age. I sobbed, placing my head on Rose's shoulder. I couldn't put up watching this happen to another beautiful little girl.

For a period of time, over the course of a few days, I sat in my room in Rose's home and asked myself if this was all my fault. Was I being punished in a perpetual circle of repeating events? Would more children die because I deserve it? I asked God what I had done wrong, why this was happening to me when I had only ever done my best as both a mother and one of his flock. I received no answers, despite how hard I begged and cried at my ceiling. Finally, after about three days, Rose returned home with Jody in a specialty wheelchair to assist her new paralysis. I did everything I could and realized that Jody was stronger than I had given her credit for. She was already developing movement in her afflicted hand and her toes would wiggle but she stated she could not feel them. Her speech was slurred, and the side of her face drooped which hurt to look at. She did not seem to notice the changes in herself.

Her prognosis became worse and worse and she developed such a hatred for life. Jody did not want to be confined to this terrible chair. She wanted to go play in the park and watch the rainbows and taste the rain and go down the slide but there was no chance for her now. One night, when we snuck downstairs for a late-night snack together, she confided in me that she no longer looked forward to growing up and wish that she didn't have to go through anymore of this pain. No more pain, no more medicine, no more struggle. She refused to make our lives harder anymore. She was sick of being alive. I burst out in tears and told her to never say that to me ever again, and that I would do anything I could to give her the gift of life back.

The next day Jody's condition worsened. Her blood pressure dropped so low that she was admitted to the hospital again. They told her mother that her outlook was grim and to expect the usual symptoms and results for low blood pressure caused by a failing heart. Rose seemed to not hear them. She seemed to be a broken woman, and in that moment, I saw myself in Rose as if I were looking at myself in a mirror. She was me, receiving the same news that I received with Olivia and she was, at this moment, realizing that she had no choice and that the rest of the dreams she had for her child would come to an end. That her child would most likely die, and that she would die with her when it happened. I held Rose's hand and knew what I had to do. This was my time to make up for my mistakes of the past and apologize to Olivia and be a better mother.

I talked to the doctors and told them that I was willing to donate my heart if they would take it and I was told the same response as before. They said that they could not euthanize me for a child simply to harvest my heart. They talked about it in such a cold way, condescending and rude, but this time I would not be stopped. I held my ground and said that if they would not take my heart on my own terms than I would, and I stormed out of the hospital that day. I went to the DMV and I changed my driver's license to ensure that I was listed as an organ donor. I went to a lawyer and adjusted my will to wish my heart off to this beautiful little girl with a whole life to live ahead of her. And then I went home.

I knew I could not drink alcohol or take any kind of drugs to mask the end, to hide it from me. They would not take my organs if I could not pass a blood test. So, because of that, I sat in my bathroom with the bathtub filled with ice. I slid into it, it's cold embrace was painful and empowering. It encouraged me to do more. I had everything I needed set up on a small table next to the bathtub and I made sure that there was enough ice available to save my body until first responders came. I made sure there would be no mess for anyone to clean up.

I dialed 911, and I told them what I was doing. The operator on the other end tried desperately to change my mind, but my blood was already staining the ice. My forearms were open for the world to see, shredded from elbow to wrist and into my hand. It didn't hurt, I was too cold when it happened, so that was a pleasant surprise. I listened to the woman wail on the phone and her plead for me to hang on just a little bit longer, and while my life essence flows out of me, I am finishing up this note. Please excuse any stains.

I want my heart to go to Jody, she needs it now more than ever. I will list the contact for the holder of my will to make sure it is executed properly. I do not want it to go to anyone else, no elderly person waiting in a line, no rich person who paid for the next available one. I want it to go to Jody. She needs it right now to make sure she grows into a beautiful woman. I want my full estate to go to Rose. I know that it isn't much, but there is some money that could support her for a bit while she stays to help Jody recover. I do not want her to work while her daughter is home alone. I want her to be well cared for and to give the best life possible for her daughter.

Finally, I want to be spread over the rainbow so that when I finally get to Heaven, I can tell Olivia what it's like on the other side. Please, I beg Jody to grow as much as possible and become as strong as she can be so that she can carry me to the top of a mountain and give me a wonderful lift off into a strong breeze as soon as a rainbow forms. I want to fly as far as I can so that I can see the whole thing, because I know Olivia is waiting to know the truth. I would like Jody to have this letter when she is older so that she can understand why the actions I chose were important to me. I never told her of Olivia directly, so this all might come as a shock. I want her to know that if she died too, I would no longer be able to live, so in an effort to save one of us, I am making this choice. It is not her fault and I am happy to do it, and if given the chance again I would not change a thing.

My body is cold, and my head is heavy now. There are no sirens, and no one is here yet, so I am glad the responders will not be here in time. I was worried when this started that I would call too soon, and they would be able to fill me back up with someone else's blood and prevent me from doing what I know I have to do. I believe I am successful, and I am so happy. I am overjoyed. I can no longer feel my fingers, the skin is turning blue and the muscles do not want to work, so I apologize for the sloppy handwriting. I am doing my best given the circumstances that bring me so much happiness. I cannot wait to see the rainbow that Jody chooses for me, because I know it will be the right one.

I am ready to see my daughter, and I am ready to give Jody a chance to have her own. Here, my letter ends, and I wish everyone well and to know that I am the happiest I have ever been. This is my goodbye.

$\mathcal{D}$ream $\mathcal{L}$etter 13
World War III

The pandemic started in early 2020 and raged through that summer. Most countries handled it well, Italy had a devastating headway of the virus, but soon got it under control. Island countries like New Zealand quickly prevented new cases altogether, but the United States; we failed entirely.

Initially the president declined that it was even happening and made it about race. He called it the "Kong Flu" in a mockery of a massive country which drove his followers into a frothing frenzy - trump followers like nothing more than a bit of racism. Trump allowed hundreds of innocent people to become sick. States had no other choice but to shut down; This infuriated the president, threatening them that he would attack in various ways if they did not reopen - he was losing money; he didn't care about American lives. The Republican Party admitted the economy was much more important than any increase of death due to the virus; They would do anything to continue their cash flow - no matter how much blood was spilled on that money.

Soon, the outbreak became uncontainable, the second wave was much more powerful than anyone could have ever imagined, and it blew the president into a twitter laden tirade. The economy shut down, his approval rating was at an all-time low, and he was embarrassed. He blamed China for all of his problems, calling them out online and instigating them to cause trouble to make them seem more like a villain than what they probably were. He wanted them to do something to boost his ratings. The twitter storm lasted for days and encompassed everything from insults to threats. He even had US military swarm around coastlines and certain bases to try and "chicken" China into acting.

Americans were busy rioting in the streets about things like the right to not wear a mask and the demand for a haircut. They said that the masks prevented them from breathing and claimed that innocent children were dying from carbon dioxide poisoning. Meanwhile, the president was selling American lives - marines were being sold off to the Russians to increase their kill count.

While he was busy golfing, hundreds of thousands of people died, yet they were all mad about masks and restaurants and their "rights" when their constitution was being defiled every single day by the president.

As mentioned before, Trump started threatening China to try and boost his rating. He egged on other countries and gained support from India who was already fighting with them due to their unfair treatment. Russia even threatened China at one point, making vague statements and accusations, anything to get the USA riled up even more than they were. No one back at home wanted it though, yet Trump persisted. One day, there was a fight that broke out at a shared Chinese/American base, shots were fired, and it became immediately aggressive. In response, China launched two bombs - nonnuclear - across the ocean. This was the longest firing attempt in the world, no one thought it would amount to anything, but Portland and Los Angeles were hit extremely hard. Hundreds of thousands of lives were lost and the country was immediately thrown into darkness. Trump called for war on the most populous country in the world and had no idea what he was doing... so they issued a draft.

I was absorbed into the draft as I had just turned 18. I was raised in the slums with my mom who could barely put food on the table, my dad worked 12 hours a day to try and keep us above water, but they always found strength through God. I swear, without that book to give me strength and encouragement, I wouldn't have made it as far as I did. When I was drafted, I packed my bag with a brand-new bible my mother had gotten for me, my name etched in gold on the spine. She kissed the cover of it and handed it to me. I will never forget that day - it was the last day I would ever see her warm face.

I was shipped to China; we were all loaded into a massive plane - filled to the brim with people - and sent overseas to occupy the country. We were dumped into Hong Kong, a location already bustling with unrest and distrust from the Chinese government. Trump was still throwing proverbial gang signs at China, still trying to drum up any support he could (it wasn't working). He was such a disgrace to the rest of the world that the Pope had to make a statement that he was causing countless and senseless death and destruction. The Pope urged him to repent and rethink his actions and to become a better person from what he was devolving into. Trump took this to heart, and instead of improving, he said that practicing religion was now illegal.

That's right - America, the USA, making Christianity illegal. People were up in arms. His usual supporters that would froth at the mouth because of his racial slurs and sexist statements were now backing away from him as if he were a plague rat. This outraged him, he was lobbing insults at the American people, saying that anyone that was against him was a Chinese supporter and assisted in the bombings on US soil. This caused civil unrest back at home, and eventually broke out into civil war.

The war at home was apparently dirty and bloody. People who already had nothing to live for were pushed into the streets and demanded change of each other, to make their world better, but others considered this a threat to their own lives and fought back. The normal selfish attitude that defined an American exploded in each person and caused mass panic. Marshall law was enacted in most states while towns resorted to minutemen militia. Immigrants were considered witches and hunted down by the American people, burning them at the stake. America was falling apart in my own very eyes and there was nothing we were able to do about it.

I landed in Hong Kong on the rainy day of July 12th, we were unloaded into a base and told to maintain the perimeter of the city. Hong Kong protestors were still occupying the area but were not considered a threat since they were fighting the same enemies. I had remembered talking to one of them about their thoughts on the USA, and they compared their fight with what the people in the US were fighting about, racial injustice and police brutality. The Hong Kong news presented, people throwing grenades at each other, civilians wearing smoke masks and innocent people being hauled away on stretchers, but now that I think about it, there is no difference between the US protests and what Hong Kong were already doing. No one wanted to admit it, but the US was controlled by brutal force, we were all just compliant enough to put up with it until the wool was pulled away from our eyes and we could finally see what was going on. The only people that didn't care were the people it was still benefiting - whites. Now that the president just made it illegal to practice religion, that tide was turning, and they too were victims.

We received notice that we were not allowed to practice our religion on the military base. Our bunks would be searched. I had hidden my bible in my mattress - not only was it the only thing holding me down to the ground, but it was the last thing I had from my mother; I had no idea if she was still alive or not. One of our draftees, Andrew, fought our commanding officer as he took his cross away - it was his wife's golden cross necklace who he left back at home. She was pregnant with their first baby and he said it still smelled like her perfume. The officer ripped it off his neck and threw it in the trash bag with everything else. Andrew was so angry, he took his standard hip knife and slit the officer's neck. In that instant I knew, I no longer cared about attacking the Chinese, they didn't ask for this and neither did we.

Later that night I was able to meet up with some draftees outside of the barracks, and we discussed about what we thought of the current establishment giving us our orders. Trump's orders were to attack any "Chinese Asian" on sight, regardless of them being in the military or not. We disagreed with that. We understood that there were bloodthirsty individuals over in the Middle East and that they were into that sort of thing, but not here. Us draftees didn't want to be here, we wanted to be home with our families. I missed mine, I knew that for a fact. We talked about our hate for the current 'dictator' in the US and decided that this wasn't for us. They couldn't control us, just because we were born on that soil did not give them the right to take away our freedom.

We made a plan to come back to our meeting spot in an hour with all of our belongings and then, after that, we would just disappear. None of us had a plan to get back home. We only had each other and faith on God that He will liberate us from this nightmare.

An hour later, I returned to our meeting spot, I had everything on my back and my bible in my back pocket. A tour vet from Afghanistan, an older boy name Tristan and I met back up. We were considered AWOL, and our veteran member told us that he had heard of people like us on his first tour - they couldn't take the environment they were put in and they fled, they were considered disgraces and laughed at; most men vowed to kill them on sight. We asked him what he thought about himself now that he was one of those people, and he said that he never had something to value so highly before, but God was always on the top of his list. Every man has a line in the sand, he said, and he wasn't about to let someone who thought they owned him cross it so easily.

We escaped; it was pretty easy. Most of the marines in the base weren't very enthusiastic. They didn't want to be there... That's what you get when you force a bunch of people who don't believe in your cause to do your bidding, you get an army who doesn't care. I knew most of the kids in our group were just that - 18 to 19-year old who were planning on going to college, who had never had a day of physical activity in their lives, now being forced into this lifestyle. It was something none of us ever wanted, and we were all equally miserable.

On the streets of Hong Kong, we fled, and into the city we were met by some civilians who took us in after initially being scared of our guns and uniforms. We held our hands up and let them search us, promising them we meant no threat. Finally, they believed us, which is by the grace of God himself, and they offered us to stay in their warehouse bunker with them. They had set up a relief station for protestors throughout the Hong Kong revolution, and had cots set up for us to sleep on. One of the civilians asked us what we were going to do now that we had nowhere to go, and we honestly hadn't thought that through. We told them we might try to go home, but they all laughed at us.

One of them pulled up a Chinese version of YouTube and showed us a video of a newsreel. On it, there were videos of the civil war taking place at home. The first video was of the national guard moving into cities and towns, taking over and removing everything that had to do with religion. They reckoned this would control the people better, so they ripped the crosses off of churches and even burned some of the structures down after tearing out the artwork and scavenging the metals inside of them. It reminded me of the Vikings that I once heard about, when they landed on the ancient islands of Europe to destroy helpless churches that were covered in gold.

Another video showed some backwoods hick, a gun slung over his shoulder, bragging about how he was going to defend his country to the death whether "they" liked it or not. The news crew asked him what he meant, and he said that Trump announced that as an American he could shoot anyone who didn't agree with him, and he was going to take that to heart. The man even aimed his shotgun at one of the members of the crew - an Asian man and asked him if he contained the virus. There was some stuttering off screen, and the gun went off, and the fat, plaid clad, greasy slob on the screen cackled like a chicken. He was so proud; he could barely talk after laughing so hard. He waved off some of the crew who were in shock to react and said that the man only lost a few toes. There was groaning and soon screaming off screen, surely as the Asian man was able to see his foot. The asshole continued to laugh.

There was a video of a man and his wife holding an assault rifle and a pistol, respectively, in their driveway, "protecting" their home from "looters". The man swung his automatic rifle around in different directions, frequently aiming it at his wife. She had her purse pistol out and walked behind her husband, often aiming it at his head. The only thing they were doing was posing a threat to themselves.

There were countless videos of police brutality - cops kneeling on African Americans, cars running people over, horses trampling innocent people, cops punching restrained protestors in the face, firing gas into obviously peaceful crowds. They asked how the protests were going, and I let them know that police coverage had fallen off topic from the news, and the civilians noted that Americans get bored quickly, and if something doesn't hold their interest anymore it basically doesn't exist. We had decided COVID didn't exist, we had decided racism didn't exist. "What was next?", they asked me, and there was no way that I could guess, a light was being shone on everything wrong in my country that I was being forced to defend. This conversation was solidifying my idea to be AWOL.

Finally, the videos turned to more riots. These were not race riots held by young African Americans and other people of color, these were riots held by white people demanding their freedom to practice their religion. They were "tired of being discriminated against" and that "Christianity has been under attack for generations now that minorities came in". There were women holding signs saying, "Let us pray again" and chanting some mind-numbing chant about their right to do whatever it is they wanted to do.

I knew I couldn't stand that nonsense for much longer and was asked again what I would do now that I wasn't with the military. I had to sit for a while and think about it, but then I asked if I would be appreciated as a Christian teacher here. The civilians seemed to mull it over, but missionaries would come from all over the world to China to attempt to convert them from their native religions. People were a little more open about allowing others to practice what they wanted, as long as it didn't harm them. There was that case, however, of Trump agreeing that the Chinese dictator should set up concentration camps against Muslims, but the civilians didn't say anything about that. The Chinese civilians had their reason to protest against their own dictator. They wanted independence and freedom.

I had asked if they wanted to go to the United States and they laughed at my comment. They asked me why they would ever want to go to a third world country? I was aghast. I had no idea what they meant. Only one clarified and said that due to the US's response to COVID that there was nothing that America could do to get them over there. Sure, their government covered a lot of it up, but at least they weren't denied healthcare or controlled in that way. I asked if that was just the way the Chinese thought of the US and they had disagreed. Apparently, we were a laughingstock to the entire world, the only thing we had going for us was our military, it was the only respectable thing left, but we were also known as high grade terrorists on the world stage. We were known to be worse than Iraq, Iran and Afghanistan. Our veteran friends were horrified and asked how that could be. They had shared information with us noting that the US took terroristic actions on Iran earlier this year, killing a general of theirs which would constitute wartime actions. They even had an arrest warrant out for Trump.

The Chinese thought America was a dangerous place to live, they thought that the police could barge in at any time and abduct you just because you weren't white. The government here showed videos constantly of US police brutality, and it almost always resulted in the person being brutally attacked, killed or abducted. I had let them know that this is exactly what we were told about China, that the police could come to their door one day and take them away simply because they spoke out on their government. We sat there for a moment and realized how similar our home countries really were.

The Chinese government just passed a law stating anyone who disagreed with their legislation could be imprisoned for life. They asked when the US would wake up from the dream they were in and do the same, fight for real freedom. I couldn't answer that question.

I sat there that night, in my bunk, looking up at the roof of the warehouse wondering how our country had fallen so far and how far it had yet to fall.

I am currently writing in the back of my Bible, in the notes section as I just found out that Russia has also taken steps against the US. Apparently, this was part of their plan for the entire world, in an attempt to obtain global control. Other countries had now joined in as well in an attempt to push the United States back to their continent and off of the Eurasian Continent. USA was now seen as the largest terrorist country in the world and was instituting the beginning of World War III.

Here I am, at 18 years old, in the middle of the Third World War. I am terrified of what my government will do to me. They already imprison anyone caught preaching or teaching gospel while religion is outlawed, and the church has no plans to do anything against the government. They have no resources to enable them to make such statement. They do note that the US is not their only source of power and if the country is going to remove religion, the only thing they will be hurting is their own people in the eyes of God. Even our churches wouldn't save us...

I do not know what I will do or where I will end up, but I know, wherever I go I will spread the word of the Lord, my Savior. It is the only thing I have the power to do now, especially in a time where we will lose more than what we have ever gained, it is a feeling of familiarity, at least to me. I do not want to see the outcome of this war or what they might do to us, but I am afraid I have no other choice but to experience it.

Tonight, the sky changed from the usual purple sunset to a shade of red I had never seen before, it was such a fiery color, some blamed it on the Asian smog, but this sky was talked about in the Bible and was predicted.

I heard a yell from the heavens above, I knew in my heart war was about to begin, God was on His way and was coming to take back the world that had fallen so far from his grace.

Dream Letter 14
The Grand Tribulation

Hello, my name is Joanne, and I thought that this might be the best way for me to tell my story. I wanted to make sure that all the information that I have learned, all of the experience that I have gone through, are stored somewhere, and I thought that this might be the best resource for that... I just want my story heard, like these wonderful stories in this book. I am not among these prophets, but my voice is still my sharpest weapon, and my words are just as sharp.

The apocalypse started in the summer of 2020, Trump had denounced the Christian faith initially in response to the Pope not supporting his attacks on China, blaming them for everything revolving around COVID and the pandemic as a whole. Many people revolted for this as Christianity is still a pillar of the American people. Now, I am not a biased woman, so I do not judge anyone based on their religion - as long as they are appreciating the higher power, whatever name they give to Him doesn't break my heart. I know His name, they know His name in their own way, we all win. Christians revolted, and he lost a huge amount of fan base for his presidency when he was already on such rocky terms from the pandemic and then the racial tensions piled on top of that. Trump tried to throw people against one another, saying that if they did not support him and the things that he was currently demanding that they were against the United States, and were terrorists. Of course, what he didn't count on was that Christians were basically the only culture that believed the government's wolf cries of "terrorist" and now that the tide was turned, they did not listen to him, and he had no support.

Soon, he said that anyone practicing any kind of religion or faith would be sentenced to jail, and he immediately pushed through a bill that did not take proper steps through the system to make it into a law. He expressed signs of clear dictatorship, and made it apparent that no laws, no regulations, nothing about the USA applied to him. We were his cow to milk, and boy was everyone mooing...

Countless members of the military had disappeared overseas. It had come to light that Russia had bought dead American soldiers to destabilize our presence; they set bounties on our men who were attempting to fight China, and that had taken another detrimental hit to the military's support of the president. Under normal circumstance the military would follow presidential command, but at the end of the day they were always expected to defend the constitution before the president. He could have bought them previously, gotten their support through money, but then he disrespected prisoners of war, and a veteran's widow by not remembering his name. Now? Now he sells off his military as target practice by Afghanistan. They no longer support him. A large percentage of American military went AWOL overseas after the draft when their religion was attacked, and still haven't been found today.

All of this happened so quickly, and now Trump is a laughingstock across the globe, but his reign has given police so much backhanded power. They can attack anyone they want who is practicing any kind of religion - giving them another excuse to target minorities. It has been insanely dangerous to try and continue a normal life anymore... I am often so scared that they will bust down my door thinking that I am a prime target. They might find my bible under my bed, and just sentence me to jail for it. I was so scared for so long that I often didn't leave the house, not that I would want to because of the plague outside. I felt like I was shuttered in, outside seemed like a raging war, people were so aggressive now. One of my neighbors had told me that they were attacked the other day because they would not take the Bible that someone was trying to force into their hands. They were asked if they were atheist, against God, and called terrible names. They were only trying to comply, just trying to get some food for their family, but this person pulled their mask down and spat directly in their face, all because they refused to join in the man's preaching about God and take a Bible.

Last week, there were a group of Muslims openly celebrating one of their many daily rituals, in a form of defiance but this prompted the ruthless wrath of the police. They launched pepper gas into the group, attempting to disperse the men as they kneeled on their mats. They were not deterred so then the police launched bean bags at them. While some men were injured initially, they were still defiant and refused to stop. Finally, the police waited until they brought their heads up from their mats and then shot them in the face with rubber bullets... I saw that firsthand, many of them lost their eyes during this devasting occasion. The men were then collected, thrown in the back of trucks and hauled off to... well... who knows where?

I finally got sick of sitting in my home letting my religion be accosted by these terrible people... My government had disgraced me with their actions, and I would no longer tolerate it. In a world that only wanted us quiet, I would not be so. All around the world people were allowed to practice their religion, I would not let that right fall here. The USA was founded on religious freedom, and I would assist in the continuation of that mindset. On day one, for me, the only thing I had was my own little Bible, the one that I had been given as a little girl at my own communion and what I have carried with me through my entire life. I took this book out into the street, and I walked for a bit (socially distanced of course). There were some people on their porches, and we talked a bit. Through our conversations I was able to find that they too were dissatisfied with the current situation. I continued my walk on down my village, and all of the conversations were the same. The next day, I decided that I had enough people that shared my thoughts. I handed them all a small slip of paper with a date and a time, and my house number on it. They all seemed quite pleased and agreed. We had just put together our first bible reading meeting.

The next day came around and I had put together as much as I could to give my best impression to my guests. I had some juice left over from one of my shopping trips. I had some small snacks to put into a bowl, but I had to remember that they were not here for my treats, but to celebrate our Lord and continue in his teachings. My first guests arrived promptly, and the rest followed soon after. After about 15 minutes we were about a dozen strong, and we read our first few passages, and had a delightfully educational conversation after. What did the passage represent for us in that time? How does a specific saying apply to our lives in the moment? It was truly wonderful, we planned to meet up three days a week. It was exactly what I needed, and I felt as if it was what my community needed as well.

We had kept this up for four weeks, a full month of learning, celebration and education. I could not express the amount of joy and purpose that this group was giving me. By our last class there were forty people coming to my house three days a week to enjoy the words of our Lord. Looking back, I suppose I did let it get a bit out of hand… I should have known that having that many people in my home, or at least visiting that frequently would draw attention from the police. We had no idea what was going to happen to us, but on our last day of our educations and celebrations, the outcome was terrible.

In the middle of a sermon one of my neighbors was giving, while we were down in the basement (our usual location to keep out of the main view of the windows) there was a massive explosion upstairs and the whole house shook over us. We had no idea what was taking place, some of us ducked trying to hide in the small spaces in the basement, but really there wasn't anywhere to hide, it was just a cinderblock basement, no closets, no alternate rooms, and no exterior doors. We were trapped like rats down here and there was no other way around it at the time... The police burst down into the room - it was terrifying because they were wearing gas masks. We pleaded for them to let us go, to be merciful, but they fired gas canisters down my basement stairs and right into us. They then slammed the door and bolted it so that we could not escape. Some of the gas that was sprayed was pepper and burned our eyes like fire. We choked and gasped and tried to find clean air but there was nothing to help us. There was no way to get a fresh breath of air and we all started to panic. Many of the older people were unconscious immediately after falling on the floor. I could barely see through my acidic tears, but I saw people dropping like flies, it was too difficult to breathe. Once the gas had affected us for long enough, and I had slumped into the corner with my Bible on my lap, it was the last thing I saw after the men in gas masks with badges came down to bag us up like livestock, or game animals that had been hunted down.

I had been loaded into a truck which is where my barely conscious head lulled me to. I was thrown against a wall, my hands and ankles tied together with zip-ties, and my face was pressed against the cold metal wall. I exasperatedly pushed myself to the side, rolled over and saw that the rest of the truck floor was stuffed to the brim with everyone from my basement. None of us were able to get out. The drive seemed like forever, there were no windows other than some slats at the top of the container we were in, and through its dim light I could see the other people waking up from the gas. Everyone coughed, all of our lungs were so badly damaged that it hurt to breath. Everyone wheezed loudly and struggled to catch their breath.

When we arrived at the containment center, we were all shoved into our own 5x5 cell, in the cell was a toilet and a bed. The back of the toilet also acted as a sink/drinking fountain. I was so out of breath, my nose and throat were so sore that I just wanted to lay down, but I couldn't even stretch out. I must have waited in that cell for a full day before a tray of slop was brought to me for a meal and after eating, I was taken to a room with a table and one chair on either side, with a mirror taking up the entire face of one wall. I could only assume it was a one-way mirror. I was sat in that room, it was probably only for an hour, but this place had no clocks for me to even tell, it felt like a lifetime. After the lifetime ended, a man came in.

He was bald and had on glasses that obscured most of his face. He sat in the chair opposite of me, and slid a glass of water within my arms reach, indicating I could have it. I took a sip, and then I was engaged in a debate into my faith. We ran through every single question ranging from "who do you celebrate" to "what would it take for you to leave your faith behind" and everything in between. It was grueling... he dug holes into every single one of my explanations, trying to unravel my beliefs and make me doubt my own ideals. I could feel what he was trying to do to me, plant seeds of doubt, seeds of conspiracy in my mind. I knew he was trying to make a garden out of me but the only thing that was planted in me by the end of that conversation was the confirmation that I had just been seated across from the devil, and he was trying to take me down. I would not be defeated so easily.

After being returned to my cell, I was held there for days. I could only see the cell directly across the row from me, and that person was changed out multiple times during my stay. At the beginning they were my peers, my neighbors but after a while they were people that I did not know. I had seen 27 people come and go, so I matched my days to the changing of the resident across the row. I had been stored here for almost a month.

Every single day the man with the glasses came to my cell and asked me what I was thinking of, and what would it take for me to change. Every single day I denied him the satisfaction of telling him that he won, that he was making a dent in my faith or destroying who I was as a person. He was relentless however… One night, when I was lumped in a ball on the bed, my idea came to me. I would trick the Devil and lie to him; tell him he had won and be set free to continue my preaching.

The next day, the man came to me, and he asked me if I had thought about what he said, and in response I told him of course I did. I had realized that perhaps my thoughts were in the wrong direction, and the man seemed smug, as the Devil would, after hearing such an admission. He asked me if there was anything else, I would like to talk about, and I told him that I didn't think I had any more ideas. He left me alone for another day.

The next day he came back and asked me if I had any more ideas. I paused, I had an entire night to think about what my statement should be, and I told him that I thought I was wrong. He smiled. He asked me if I would like to go home, and I told him I would like nothing more. He flicked through a folder that he kept under his arm on the other days and handed me a photo. My house number was written on the bottom corner, but the only thing in the picture was a small pile of rubble. He said that everyone in my party admitted that I was the center of the Bible study, so while they were willing to release me, they could not have me returning to my base of operation. He said that this is the consequence for my defiance of the president's law, and that next time, if I was caught practicing, I would be killed. I could barely hear him as my tears flowed so heavily and my sobs were so deep, I could barely breathe.

I was told to put my wrist through the door of my cell, and he would prepare me for leaving. I was so upset, I cooperated but before I knew it, a scream was all I could utter - the bastard had branded the inside of my wrist with a cross of Christ himself! He said that I was now labeled that I had been captured once for the practice of Christianity and that this would be an indication that the next time, I was captured I would be disposed of. I reeled in pain, on my tiny little cot, and soon another worker came through and forced me out of the cell. Someone was already being led into it, and the door slammed behind me and onto someone else.

I was forced out of the building into another truck where the back was completely blacked out and I was transported back to where my "home" was. I was dropped off right at where my doorstep would be, but the smell of burning wood was still fresh in the air. I had nothing else to do, nowhere else to go and I was devastated. I sat for the rest of the afternoon on the curb by my house and sobbed. None of my neighbors had the balls (without any other way to say it) to come help me, or even talk to me. No one spoke to me, but I could see their curtains shimmer as they looked at me out of their living rooms or foyers. I felt so disgraced by these ungrateful people. Finally, the sun set on my shame, and I finally felt the strength to stand up. My legs had suddenly discovered purchase on the pavement, and I knew what I had to do.

The Bible gave me all the strength in the world. Jesus was killed for his mission, and so will I as long as I have God in my heart. I pulled up my bootstraps, now that I was in the only set of clothing I owned, and I decided to move south. I knew I could teach there... but what if the north needed me? If the south was flooded with religion, then perhaps the north was my location... To clear my mind, I just walked.

I walked street after street in no definable direction, and eventually I found myself moving north. The lord knew where I had to go and where I would be appreciated the most, but also where I would be put into the most danger. I continued walking for days and days, my feet began to blister, and I could feel the soles of my shoes loosen on the bottom. I felt my skin blister from the sun, and I often found strands of my hair fall to my shoulders. I didn't know the last time I had water, but I knew I had to go wherever I dropped.

And drop I did! I landed in a little north eastern town where everyone was quiet and secluded but the area looked as if they had lost God before the outbreak and the ban on religion took place. The houses were disheveled, no homes that God blessed were here, so gently I went around and knocked on doors. People were hesitant to open up, but once they did, I was allowed into their abodes and began to preach. The people gave me water, some offered me food, and a family even offered me some ointment for my skin and some new clothing to replace the stuff that had degraded with exposure to the sun. I did not stay in this town, but I moved from home to home, and each time someone let me in they were always open with kindness and generosity. I knew that those were the people that would let me preach to them, and they often said I helped them.

Moving from home to home brought me into a large city, and more and more people let me in, and continued to supply me with what I needed. They often offered me access to a bed, or to shower in their home. I was always amazed at the generosity of my growing flock. Soon, people joined me moving from place to place, and together we would fan out into towns and do the same thing, just talk to anyone who would allow us to. Finally, we entered Philadelphia, our group was so large we were able to enter many homes a day to preach about our Lord and Savior. We took to the streets, and when the police attempted to stop us, we stood and did not relent. Their gasses could not stop us, and their attacks could not hinder us. We even created shields out of plywood to bounce back gas canisters to them, and eventually those shields were stopping rubber bullets. Some of our people were injured, but those in the city helped us with their own skills - medics and even veterinarians helped to tend to our wounds, joined our cause and pushed us on.

I am writing this note as we come close to an end. The news indicated recently that all religion practices will be abolished worldwide. No one was allowed any longer to talk about their faith. Concentration camps were built to separate all religion just like the Holocaust. Unfortunately, they caught up with me. Jews were separated, Jehovah Witness were separated, Catholics were separated, and most Muslims were killed rather than thrown into concentration camps. Many people were losing their lives, and I can feel Gods wrath coming close. The government are now making innocent people regret their beliefs and if they do not, they were shot down and killed. The camps are overpopulating, and I sit here waiting for my row to be called next, they want to burn us alive, but I am not sure if they will succeed. As I look out the window, the bright blue sky is now turning red, and a loud trumpet can be heard from the heavens above, with a scream of anger. I knew God will save us. Today is His day.

Dream Letter 15
Armageddon

I am currently sitting in the wreckage of my old office, cowering under my own desk. My office is in the middle of Times Square, I am on the 56th floor and I can overlook the city in its entirety. I am hiding now, and I wanted to write this letter just in case I am unable to make it off of this floor or out of this building. I wanted to tell my family, if they will ever find this letter, that I am sorry for the man that I have been up to this day. Meredith, my wife, I am sorry that I was so cruel to you over the years when you were only trying to raise our children the best way you could on your own. Lord knows I didn't help at all, and I am sorry. To my sons I am sorry that I was never the father that you wanted me to be, no ball games, no car work, no life advice. You only saw my worst side, and it got increasingly worse over the years with the drinking. I am sorry to all of you, and if you find this letter that means that I never came home. I can only hope that my apology written on paper is worth a fraction of an apology spoken directly to you - because that is what you all deserve.

It started early this morning. I had only just gotten into the office; I was angry that I had rode up on the elevator with the custodian. I had always thought that those types of people should have their own elevator, so we didn't have to see them... I know that I was being cruel. I snatched my schedule out of my secretary's hand, I didn't even say good morning to her, I just told her to get me a coffee from the shop on the fourth floor. I threw all of my shit onto the chair next to my door and slammed it behind me as hard as I could, I wanted everyone in the office - both above and below - to know that I was in for the day, and I wasn't about to take anyone else's garbage. I went over to sit in the big leather chair I had bought myself, I wanted something that would look amazing behind my cherrywood desk (yep, the very one that may become my coffin). I flopped into the chair and leaned back as far as the springs could take me, propping my heels up on my desk. I was feeling pretty good being me, at that time, and I skimmed through my schedule. I got pissed because my secretary had filled it up again. I am a writer and an editor, so why does she feel the need to run me directly into the ground every single day? I took a red pen and I scratched tons of stuff off of my day. About the time I was finishing up, she came back in and set the drink down on my desk. Iced hazelnut double café late with two shakes of cinnamon. At least she could do something right. I threw the schedule at her and told her to get rid of the things that I crossed out. If she didn't like it, I told her she could handle them herself or get out of my office. She left, I gave her direction now, a goal, a consequence. What more could she ask for? Back up went my feet, and I put my hands behind my head like a cradle. I enjoyed my drink.

Time stood still for a little while; I didn't notice it at first. It was silent in the office outside when there are normally grunts running all over the place making a mess of themselves and causing all kinds of annoying commotion. It was too quiet... No one was out there. What the hell? We are only three weeks being back from quarantine. Did everyone just decide that they needed another four months off from work? Well, I knew I wouldn't be paying their unemployment so they can all kiss their desks goodbye and pick out a nice spot on the sidewalk outside - maybe they would have some luck as beggars? I got up out of my chair and opened the door to the bullpen outside, expecting to see an empty office.

Everyone was there, but instead of working they were all lined up by the windows looking outside from it. I was astonished at their insubordination. Why would they all be dicking around like this, wasting MY money? I stormed out of my office, my door hitting the wall in the office hard enough to dent the drywall, and I started screaming. I don't know what I was saying, probably something along the lines of "get your asses back in these desks and get my stories to me before lunch" or "I didn't know I hired a bunch of window lickers, we can make you window cleaners in a heartbeat". The usual. No one seemed to care at all about my yelling. This outraged me. I didn't like being ignored, I wasn't on this planet to be ignored, and I could feel my blood pump in my ears as they all continued to ignore me. I slammed on a nearby desk to try and get their attention, but no one turned around. Soon, I felt someone standing next to me. It was my secretary, I almost wrung her neck - at least she did something today, that saved her from the punishment.

I had asked her what all these assholes were doing, and she told me to come over with her and look out the window. What? Now they expected me to waste my time watching the rats down on the street? Whatever... I went over with her. She pointed down at the ground, East, and everyone on the street was looking in that direction as well. I could see a strong breeze coming from that direction – dirt, dust and trash was being whipped around. Women held their hair out of their face and men held their hats on their head. I asked her what the fuck I was supposed to watch - some wind? She told me to keep watching. Everyone continued to watch.

The wind did pick up harder and harder, the sky was turning pink - like an early summer sunset although it was only just past 8am. The color deepened and soon became as red as blood, reflecting that same light over everything and making outside seem eerie and grotesque. The wind was lashing now, small signs were ripped off their posts and thrown into buildings. I could see cars rocking on their tires - the smaller sedans seemed to be barely able to hold onto the ground, and on one particularly strong gust a few did flip over. The wind stayed coming from the east, and it continued to get stronger and stronger the longer it went on. I asked her if this was a hurricane. It was early for hurricane season, and they rarely came up the east coast far enough to cause any kind of commotion in the city. She said she didn't know; the weather was clear this morning. All of the workers were just as stunned as I was, and I looked at them watching the weather outside, the eerie red glow reflecting on their faces, casting gloomy shadows on them, making them look old and haggard.

I asked them if I paid them to look at the weather, and what they actually got paid to do, but they just looked at me, with an angry expression on their faces, the red light making it all more dramatic. This made me angrier, I didn't pay them to judge me, that wasn't how our agreement worked. They worked for me, I owned them, they had no right to look at me like that. I started screaming about them wanting their jobs and if they didn't, they could leave. There was a shared look among them and slowly, one by one, they started filing out of my office. I was gob smacked. How dare they! I screamed and screamed, I told them I would slash every single benefit they had, no unemployment for them, no insurance, nothing. I'd get a lawyer to sue them for last month's wages since our profits were down, I kept screaming until my office was empty. Only my secretary and the office kiss ass were left. I was so pissed; I could only stand with my hands on my hips while my face cooled off. My secretary handed me a glass of water and I drenched my hand and ran it down my face to try and cool off. The yes man looked back out the window and his expression turned to shock. Over a little wind? I looked too.

The wind was something else now, there were clouds that you couldn't quite make out the contents of, but they would swarm people, everything would disappear among the clouds, and then when it moved on to the next group, some people would be left standing, some people would be laying on the sidewalk. It moved through Times Square, multiple foggy patches taking out so many people. I could only assume that the people on the sidewalk were dead. Those who remained stood, their arms over their head protecting themselves from the wind as they continued to try and hide from whatever was happening.

I saw a few foggy balls smash through the bottom of the neighboring building, and at about the same time there was a vibration in our own, probably the same thing happening. The three of us looked at each other, and I watched the other building, as the fog moved up floors. The yes man and the secretary both took shelter under their desks. I watched the fog come up to just below our level as I urged the other two to come to me, and both my employees came closer, we stood in the bullpen, the wind had entered this office now, and papers were lashing throughout the entire room. I watched the fog in the other building reach our level, and when I looked back, the fog for our building had just entered ours. It rushed us, and lingered. I knew what this was…

I fell to my knees and began praying. I apologized for all of the bad things I had ever done, for the bad person I had become. My secretary didn't know what I was doing, but she knelt next to me, the yes man stood and watched through the fog. I prayed and repented for my sins, and my secretary soon caught on and did the same thing. She clasped her hands in front of her as tightly as she could, her knuckles were white. My hands were flat on the floor, my head hung as I begged for the Lord's forgiveness. I repeated and repeated my apologies, I acknowledged my wrongdoings and how I planned to fix them, and right about when I went to refill my lungs, I looked up at the man next to me. He was frozen stiff, his eyeballs were completely scorched from his head, only the black remains of char were left on his skin. He wasn't pure enough to look at the creature which had entered my office… His body was like a board, standing up only because it hadn't been pushed down yet. I felt something near me, and I once again looked at the ground. I did not want to risk the same fate happening to me. The thing lingered on the two of us, it waited, it judged. It left.

As soon as the fog left the room, the yes man's body fell to the floor in a ragged heap. The secretary screamed at the sight of it, his eyeless face was twisted and gnarled as if it had aged a hundred years in only the minute or two that we were examined. His youth was taken, his life was removed from him, the being took back the essence that made him "him", and not a rock or a piece of moss or something. The fog completely left moving towards the other floors, I watched the other building go through the same thing, floor after floor, past our own. The secretary asked me what just happened and why "John" was dead. John? I guess that's what his name was; I thanked Jesus and the Lord for giving me my life to learn that bit of knowledge about my once-was peer.

I told her it was an angel. She said she didn't see anyone when the thing was nearest to us, and I glared at her. I told her most people didn't survive looking at an angel, their purity was often too much for the human eye. I pointed at John on the floor as an example. She said she still didn't see anyone, it was just thick fog, just the whitest mist she had ever seen in her life. I told her angels weren't represented as people until later in the Bible, and their true form was an omnipresent being without shape or sound. Sometimes the Bible referenced them as a mound of eyes, all seeing, with a thousand wings - but that was most likely someone's creative flare. She asked how I knew all of this, and together we went into my office. In the top shelf of my desk, I threw out all of the paperwork and garbage I had stuffed in there, and at the very bottom was a small bible with golden page edges. I handed it to her. I told her that when I first got this job, I was a God-fearing man, but as I grew, I became the man that was to be feared, God had no part in my life, I made my own successes. He only brought the negatives. Plus, with the new illegalization of religion, it sort of solidified my ideals. She flicked through some of the well-worn pages. She said she hadn't opened her Bible since her mother died and blamed the Lord for taking her away, but when she was kneeling, she felt the power that He often gave to her when they were sitting in mass. She recited all the words she could remember, and she said she felt that was what saved her life. She asked why angels were on Earth and what they were doing, why were they killing people?

These are the end of times, I knew this. I was so sure of it. So many people would die - nonbelievers and false followers would be culled. I told her that was most likely why John was killed out of all of us. She asked me why I was not, I was not a nice man, why would I be spared? This hurt my feelings, but I realized she was correct. I told her it was because in my moment of reckoning I repented, I apologized for my sins. I promised to become a better man. She shook her head at me, judged me, asked me if I meant it. I told her I did. I even asked her what her name was - for the first time after four years of working together. Her name was Stephanie.

There was a strange sound outside, and Stephanie and myself went over to the window in my office where we were able to see the west side of town. The sky was still blood red, but in it a scar had formed. It was lined with yellow and the laceration itself was black - like a festering wound. It was slashed from the highest point in the sky to the horizon as if a massive blade had come down and done it, ripped the sky open from ear to ear, and out of it spewed more fog, lumps of fog flowed out of the wound and came crashing down on earth, and after a few moments, we were able to see something else come through.

I grabbed the binoculars. Horsemen came through the opening and they were all very distinctive. The first horse was as white as freshly fallen snow, and atop it sat Jesus himself, come to Earth to do his father's bidding and reap his wrath. He had a sword in his hand, the hilt of gold and the blade of copper that had turned blue through the millennia.

The next horse came through in a cloud of fog, this one was chestnut, but its coat resembled the color of the sky - angry and red. The horse itself was thick and muscular, matted fur ringed its feet and its bobbed tail lashed back and forth. Atop this horse sat a Roman gladiator, his face coated in the blood of his rivals who he was destined to slay. His bronze armor shone in the red light like molten lava, and the crest of red horsehair on his helmet made him look frightening. He was a massive man with muscles to spare and he carried a heavy pilum, a long and thin needle like spear for throwing, that he lobbed at people on the ground, which would always return to his hand.

The third rider came in on a horse so black that its fur did not shine from any kind of light. It was a nimble creature, with elegant and long features that were partially covered by its riders equally black robes. Death sat atop this hose, his skull face peeking out of his hood every now and again as he opened his mouth to consume the souls of the fallen. The angels existed as a white fog, where when death would conjure souls from the dead and the damned, they would be removed from bodies as black smoke. They flowed into him, and wherever he went he had more to swallow.

The final horse was sickly. It was a dun with bare bones features. All of its ribs were showing, and from its exposed pelvis bones hung cages, filled with dead animals, swaying at its hips like trophies. Every vertebra in its neck could be seen as its main; the tail had fallen out unevenly due to starvation. It's fur even had a sickly green tinge to it despite the reddened sky. Hunger rode this horse, he was a skeleton himself, only clothed in skin - just enough to keep his bones from the air, but not enough to hide any of them. He followed war and Jesus through the city, as the two of them created havoc in the streets. Death was right behind the three of them, capturing the souls of each of their victims.

People were lost in the square now. Angels were still going from place to place to weed through the easiest of targets. The rest would have their worth determined by Jesus himself. That meant that Stephanie and I too would be judged when they came around. I turned to the poor girl and let her know that while we might have survived our first reckoning, we very well might not survive the next. Jesus himself does not hear our prayers or our calls to forgiveness, he only sees our souls and their worth, how much they are weighed down with the weight of our wrongdoings. That is how we will be judged when he arrives, and if he does not find us to be worthy his sword or the Roman's pilum will be the last thing we feel before our souls are ripped from our chests and consumed like a meal fit for a king. I could see the fear on her face, I could see the agony of the realization of what might happen. She asked me what she could do, she had a baby at home with her husband - how could she return to them? I told her I did not know, but she might as well leave now to try. They will find her regardless of where she goes as the beings are all knowing, so an effort has to count for something. She looked at me for a long while, then outside where the rampage was happening and nodded. She understood what she had to do, wished me the best she could, and left the office. The door closed quietly behind her. That would be the last I would ever see her, and I had only just learned her name and that she had a family.

That is how I ended up under my desk. When she left, all that remained with me was my sudden realization of my loneliness. Was my family safe at home? Were my boys trapped at school through this? Was my wife minding the house alone to have these things come and destroy her? ...Were they thinking of me in the same way? Did my kids care enough about me to wonder if I was safe? Was my wife wondering if she would be a widow? I couldn't imagine any of them cared about me, I am such a terrible person to them, and I know that I most likely will never be able to make that up. In my fear, I walked over to my cherrywood desk and crawled under it. I pushed myself into the very corner of the desk, and I sobbed loudly. I cried for my family. I cried for myself. I cried for my own stupidity and selfishness and cruelty over the years. I really was sorry for the way that I had acted, and I knew that if given the chance, I would make things right again. I would try as hard as possible for that. But that chance was so slim. I most likely would not be spared.

I could now hear screaming as the horsemen drew closer to the building. I knew that this was in response to the Global release of religion. God knew that the world had thrown religion away, in favor of war and havoc and mayhem. In response to our disobedience he has now brought war to us and his counterpart, hunger, for us to have a final taste of our own medicine. We had been a warmongering, terroristic country for far too long and removing religion was the final straw of it all. We would no longer be tolerated.

I heard the familiar vibrations in the building I was in. Something had entered again and this time I could not be so certain that it was an angel. I knew that if it was, I would be lucky and that I was already spared by their hivemind, I would not be touched by another one. God, however, knew that deep down in my soul I had a lot to make up for - why give that person a life knowing that he did wrong all these years. Why not spare someone like Stephanie with the world at her feet and her future as her road, a family growing as strong as an oak tree? She could be dead on the 20th floor for all I know, if they killed her, then they would certainly kill me. I kept praying in my little cave.

I knew that if I was going to die in the most critical way possible, I was not going to do it sober. I glugged on that bottle until I heard screaming in the floor below, and I looked out my window, which was like a massive TV screen, where I could see the reflection of this building in the window of the other. I could see what was happening in the lower floors. I saw the flash of the blue blade and the smear of blood on glass. Every once in a while, the perfected spear would lunge into view, through the body of someone who was lucky enough to avoid angelic judgement, but not lucky enough to have a soul light enough to appease Jesus himself. I could hear the horse hooves downstairs as they trampled desks and technology and smashed through dividing walls and barriers. I could feel it rear and buck as its whole weight came crashing down on the floor below it. The group came nearer and nearer to where I was hiding.

I saw the horses climb the floors of my building, the glistening white reflection of our lord and savior's horse was unmistakable in the dark reflection, I could never be mistaken as I watched my death ride nearer. I felt my palms dampen, they made holding the bottle so much harder than it had to be. I took another long drink of the foul fluid. My heart started racing and I could feel the painful thumping in my throat. I felt my stomach sink as the white horse passed on the level directly below my own. I felt my stomach light on fire with the alcohol and the fear, and I felt goosebumps develop all over my skin. I heard the thumping outside my office, and I felt such an immense pressure come near me, something that I could not explain. It felt as if my body was being weighed down under a ton of bricks, my limbs felt exhausting to move, yet they still could. My chin wanted to rest against my chest, but I drug it up, to look out of my hiding spot.

As I watched, I felt an insidious cold chill wash over me, and a black dusty fog seeped into my room. I could watch each particle swirl around on the carpet and the color of the steam thickened as its owner neared me. I felt the footsteps come closer and could feel them press heavily down into the padded office carpet. Finally, I saw the pointed black shoes of death step in front of me, his long robes splashing around on the carpet. He waited, momentarily, until he dropped to his knees like a sack of potatoes. In front of me was the face of death - it was a silver skull adorned with many scars and marks of lashing prey. The mouth hung open as the creature looked at me, the demigod seemed confused by what he was seeing as his eyeless skull looked me over. I waited for my soul to be sipped from my body, and I wondered if it was painful. He continued to watch, until he stood once again and turned. I could hear the tackle of another horse jingle and its rider dismounted. The pressure in the room grew heavier and heavier, until a pair of bare feet were now standing in front of me. A hand reached down, and two fingers flicked, indicating I was to stand but my body was so heavy I didn't think I was capable. Without my thinking, and certainly without my consent, my body did his bidding and I crawled out from my hiding spot and stood before Jesus himself. He looked smugly at me. He said he thought I had learned much today. He said he watched me fall into the life that I had been in just yesterday and he was initially disappointed in me and didn't think that I was capable of being a better person. He was glad that his apocalypse had brought about a change in me and prompted me to take up my Bible again. He said he was proud of me, at least that counted for something.

My body was still heavy, and I could not move, though I stood in front of Jesus himself as if floating on my toes. War strode up beside him, the bulging muscles coated in gore, stood next to him, contrasting his clean white clothing beautifully. Jesus spoke softly, but he said he was choosing a select few humans to continue to speak his name, only those who show true faith would be allowed to continue. I, apparently, was capable of changing and growing as a person and I was expected to carry on Christianity in his namesake. I swallowed hard and he gave me such a gentle touch on my shoulder, it felt as if my entire being had been lightened from the burdens that held it down for so many years. My age disintegrated and I felt rejuvenated. I could not believe it...

The deities and Jesus himself left, climbing the floors of my building where I heard more screams. I sprinted towards the window just one more time before leaving, a louder scream was heard from the heavens above, and large balls of flames were striking down the city, destroying all the buildings it touched. Heavy rain followed and the wind picked up even faster. Lightning strike down as well, the United Nation was destroyed as the flames burned down all the flags. Everyone knew who was winning this war. God made Himself clear. Today was His day, His day of judgement. Soldiers aimed their riffles and fired their bullets into the sky, but to only be met with the sword of Jesus himself.

I am going to try and find my family, as Jesus said that I could recover what I love most and take it with me on my journey. I am leaving this note, this story of what happened here today in case I don't make it. In case some angel feels I am no longer valuable enough to live, in case God himself cracks through the sky and decides He is done with humanity altogether. I love my family, I am coming for you, and I want you to know I will be a changed man.

Dream Letter 16
Angel's Dream

I remember the airport that night, it was dark and gloomy, and I was mostly alone. I saw no one else as I waited for my flight from the MCO airport in Orlando to New York City. I sat in my chair, my bag at my feet and my phone plugged in while I scrolled mindlessly to pass the time. All of a sudden, I felt the hair on the back of my neck prickle to attention. My pupils dilated and I looked away from my screen. No one was in front of me, no one had come in, but when I looked over my shoulder, in the corner, a heavy shadow lingered. It was darker than the other corners and seemed more of an eerie darkness than what should be in an airport. I tried to distract myself from it, but the uneasiness persisted. I closed my eyes in an attempt to blink the feeling away, I clenched them together, wishing the discomfort to be gone.

I kept my eyes closed for a few moments to clear the feeling, but when I opened them, I was displaced. I was sitting in a train car in the city, outside whizzed past impossibly fast. The shadow still loomed in the corner. I watched it and I could feel it watching me, filling me with discomfort and fear. I got up and tried to leave the car, go somewhere more comfortable, away from this thing but it followed.

I picked up my pace and ran from car to car, passing between each one and slamming the door behind me, but the thing followed, not bothering to open the door to move through it. Without warning, I felt the train come to a screeching stop and it flung me forward into a seat. The thing neared me. The announcer noted us that this was 174th street and the doors opened. I threw myself into the freedom outside, into New York City and lunged down the steep stairway that lead to the train platform. I leapt the admission bars and exited the train station. Like a prey animal I felt the shadow drawing ever closer to me, keeping up with me impossibly well.

Standing just outside of the train station, a place that I should not be, I saw things that I had not seen in years. I should have been back at the MCO airport, but instead I saw my childhood school. Feeling my pursuer edge ever closer, I began to run. I sprinted past my family's church and could practically see us in the window standing for hymn. Taking a tight turn, I passed by the park where I learned how to swing on the monkey bars, I saw bus 36 - my high school bus - speed by to make its next stop. This all weighed me down with a heavy feeling of nostalgia that lured me into stopping once or twice, but the overpowering pressure from this shadow pushed me forward. I kept running.

I passed my best friend's house, and I could see our sidewalk chalk drawings tangling around my feet like they were grabbing at my shoelaces. I could smell the doughnut shop before I could see it, its open doors and golden glow inviting me in to have a doughnut and preach with my family. My head was spinning violently at everything I was seeing, and when I closed my eyes and shook my head to try and steady myself, I was back at the foot of the train station, just off of the massive staircase leading to the platform again, as if I had not gone anywhere. The shadow was closer than ever, almost within reaching distance. With a pinch in my heart I lunged away and sprinted back down the Main Street. I felt my life was truly in danger from this shapeless figure.

I ran and ran, my feet pounding loudly on the inner-city pavement, I shoved people out of my way and shouted at them to clear the path and let me through. I ducked under a set of scaffolding and skipped back and forth between the steel piping that held it up, looking over my shoulder to see if I lost the monster. It persisted. Breaking out of the dark understory and into the city light I came into view of a reflective building. I saw myself running, thought it seemed as if I was running on a treadmill, the glass wall giving me a clear view of myself never seemed to end. I saw the exhaustion in my face and redness in my cheeks and stress in my eyes. I could also see the shadow getting closer, hot on my heels. I had no idea where to go, the only place I knew was to go home. Where my parents were. Where my family was. This was the only place that I could expect safety and protection from this demon.

The Bronx was at the top of a steep hill and I could feel my lungs in my chest as if I had swallowed a match. They burned and ached and threatened to split apart like overripe fruit if I dared to take one more breath. I dared. My legs quivered at each step when my foot was free from the pavement, my thighs protesting each lurch forward. My arms started to weaken and drop from holding them at chest level, but I could see it! The top of the hill was so close!

I made it! Surely the monster couldn't have pursued me all the way up here. I put my hands on my knees and took some much-needed gulps of air, stealing it away from the rest of the world. As I knelt down, I looked between my knees and saw the sky, and the shadow almost on top of me! I broke away and forward again! Passing the local Domino's, I felt a little rejuvenated from having a second to catch my breath, but I was already running out of steam. The building complex was so close though! It was only a little bit further! I could see it! Still, I ran.

I slammed myself against the door, my hand hitting the admittance button. I pounded against it over and over again, urging someone to take my call to let me up. A very familiar voice came over the intercom and asked me who was there. I told him it was me, his younger brother and to let me in! I urged him; it was to save my life. He allowed it, and I felt the door unlock. Right before the shadow could reach me, I threw the door open, jumped inside and slammed it shut behind me with both arms. Panting as heavily as I thought possible, I ran up the stairs to the second floor "2R".

My older brother was waiting for me with the door open and he let me into our childhood home. I breathlessly told him what had happened and how far I had ran, and the visions I saw. He listened silently and attentively but interrupted me to let me know that no one is following me. For a moment I was astonished but perhaps he didn't see the shadow creature… I didn't care. I finally felt secure and safe. The creature didn't come through the door to my home. It didn't follow me into the lift. It didn't pursue me anymore. I finally felt a little comfort in my heart and the giant cloud of dread went away. I saw my sisters in another room, they were singing along to their favorite song. My older brother was in the living room noisily playing his beloved PS3. My father was in the kitchen sitting in his favorite red velvet chair smoking a Marlboro while talking to my mother and my third brother as they were cooking at the stove.

I needed to cool off, I excused myself and went into the bathroom to splash some water on my face. How did I get here? My head was spinning. I washed quickly and patted my face with a soft and well-worn bath towel. When I opened my eyes and looked into the mirror, I didn't see myself. I saw who I was ten years ago, a young me stared back, eyes filled with hope and joy and laughter. My scraggly toothed mouth was a giant smile and I couldn't help but match it. I patted my cheek and felt soft young skin under my hand.

I left the bathroom and went into my mother's room where the window overlooked the front of the building where I left the shadow creature. I looked down, and saw the creature standing outside of the door but this time, as I watched it, I did not feel the same doom and gloom that had chased me all the way here. I felt a sense of strong security as if I had been pacified. A bright light flashed, causing me to blink, and when I looked back down to the shadow, in its place I saw an angel standing there. The man with wings as glorious as clouds on a summer day protected the building door with a staff made of gold. I focused on the light shining off of the glorious weapon, it was startled by the announcement over the airport intercom...

I was awoken rudely by the announcer calling my flight number and boarding instruction. I was sitting back in the MCO airport in the thick Florida air. With confusion cemented on my face, I looked over my shoulder where the shadow was the first time; It was no longer there. I was truly alone here besides for the man who was attending the boarding counter. In the corner of my mind I could hear my mother, back in the day when I fled a childhood home, telling me I couldn't run away from my past, she said it would always follow me no matter where I went. Begrudgingly I stood, tossing my bag onto my shoulder and neared the boarding host. Such a strange feeling I thought, but why now after so many years?

Perhaps the shadow that was following me and filling me with such terror was my past? I could never outrun it, no matter how hard I tried unless I returned to where I needed to be. I handed over my ticket to the attendant, lost deeply in my thoughts. Home was the only place where a person actually felt comfortable and safe... Maybe this creature was meant to show me that no matter what I did I wouldn't be able to move toward my "to be" without finishing my "has been". I rubbed the back of my head as if a heavy weight had just been lifted off of me, but the void created was just filled with rushing waves of confusion. Somehow, I knew that creature, the angel, standing outside of my childhood home would always be there to protect me, to be prepared for me, for whatever my future may bring so long as I kept my past in my vision too.

Printed in the United States
By Bookmasters